THE BEAST IN A SUIT

EVERNIGHT PUBLISHING ®

www.evernightpublishing.com

ELENA KINCAID

Copyright© 2019

Evernight Publishing

Editor: Karyn White

Cover Art: Jay Aheer

ISBN: 978-1-77339-936-2

THE BEAST IN A SUIT

DEDICATION

I would like to dedicate this book to the members of my Sinfully More Erotic Street Team, aka, SME, especially to three very lovely ladies, Rhonda, DeAnne, and Christina, whose names appear throughout the book. To Maia Dylan and Sarah Marsh, my two writing partners and who, along with myself, make up SME, I love you girls. To many more projects together!

THE BEAST IN A SUIT

THE BEAST IN A SUIT

A Contemporary Tale, 1

Elena Kincaid

Copyright © 2018

Prologue

"Once there lived a boy in a castle. He was all alone with no parents or friends to speak of, trapped inside the confines of the property. He could hear the cackles of the witch who cursed him echoing in the hallways almost every night. And every time, the little boy would run to an open window, place his hands over his ears, and scream. Only when it was over did he finally go to bed. 'Good night, Mama. Goodnight, Papa,' he'd say to their framed portraits hanging on the wall directly in front of his bed. In the winter months, when the winds picked up and howled, he'd pretend it was his mother singing him to sleep."

"Marguerite, isn't there a more pleasant story you can tell our child at bedtime?" Emeline's father asked, pausing in the doorway of her bedroom. He looked almost comical with his round, rimless glasses sitting at the tip of his nose as he peered over them at his wife, his curly mop of brown hair wildly disheveled, more than likely from running his hands through it as he often did.

"But I love this story, Papa," Emeline said in French. "And it has a happy ending." She glanced at her mother, who gave her a surreptitious wink. They both knew how to play her father. She switched to English. "And furthermore, I would think as a literary professor, you would appreciate the importance of the feminist undertone. The male protagonist is essentially rescued by a damsel, and *he* is the one in distress."

Her father barked out a laugh as he stepped into her room. "Are you absolutely certain, Mama, that she is only eight?" he asked her mother.

"You were there when she was born, dear." Marguerite shook her head.

Being the daughter of a French-born father and an Italian-born mother, while residing in the United States, resulted in Emeline being fluent in three languages, and long before she had any understanding of what being trilingual meant. They sometimes bantered back and forth in three different languages, though her father, when not teaching, often favored French.

"A changeling, then," her father continued teasingly. He sat on the bed and began to tickle her mercilessly. "They switched our daughter out for this forty-year-old stuck in a child's body."

Emeline's peals of laughter were from both being tickled and her father's theories about her. She let her imagination run wild, picturing herself as this changeling child and living in a far-off land where magic lived and thrived. Perhaps *she* would be the one to save the boy from the evil witch.

Her mother poked her father in the ribs. "Stop it, Edmund, or she will never go to sleep."

"But he's right, Mama," Emeline said as soon as

her father had ceased his tickling. "I'm a fairy princess, ancient and wise, and if you ever want to see your real daughter again, you must pay me with a thousand chocolate bars."

This time both her parents went in for the attack. A few giggle fits later, her strength as well as the strength of her parents had waned. She wouldn't get the end of the story tonight. No matter, though. She had memorized it all, but she would have begged her mother to finish it in her beautifully melodious Italian accent had she known her mother would never have the chance to tell it to her again.

Her father kissed her sweetly on her forehead. "Sweet dreams, *mon ange*." Her mother followed suit, then tucked her daughter in before standing up. Emeline, however, had one more kiss she wanted to deliver. She touched her mother's rounded belly before closing her eyes and kissing it softly. She silently promised to be the best big sister ever.

When Emeline opened her eyes again, she found herself alone. Darkness surrounded her. The only sound she heard was that of a baby crying. She ran blindly, trying to get to it, but every time she came close enough to expect to find the source of the crying, the sound once again carried from a distance. "Where are you?" Emeline yelled. "Please … where are you?" she ended on a whisper.

"Wake up."

Her body shook, and then she heard the voice again telling her to "Wake up."

Chapter One

Emeline bolted into a seated position, dislodging the hand she felt on her shoulder. "What ... where?" Confusion set in as she took in her surroundings. The smell of dirt and grass, as well as a woodsy male cologne, penetrated her nostrils.

A man stood up from his crouched position, towering over her, the sun behind him obscuring her vision, making her squint. He was huge, well over six feet, and very muscular. A sudden fear settled into her, mixing with her current state of disorientation.

"Do you often sleep in cemeteries?" the deep, velvety voice asked her. He had an English accent, though not very pronounced. "Do you know how dangerous it is?" He continued chastising her without waiting for a response to his first question. "Anyone could have..." He gestured around him with his hand instead of finishing his sentence.

"And you're not dangerous?" Emeline asked as she stood up and brushed herself off. His questioning finally permeated her brain, snapping her out of her haze. She was in a cemetery, only now it was broad daylight. She'd had trouble sleeping last night, tossing and turning, knowing what a hard day today would be for her and her father, until she gave up on sleep altogether. She got in her car, the one she pretty much only used on weekends when she drove from her apartment in Manhattan to her father's house in Long Island, and arrived at the cemetery where her mother and stillborn brother were buried. It had still been dark out.

"I *could* be dangerous," the stranger replied.

He stepped closer to her, blocking out the sun and allowing her to finally see his face clearly. Striking emerald eyes peered down at her, momentarily holding her in place. Long black lashes encircled his piercing gaze, framed by thick, dark-blond expressive eyebrows. They were furrowed at the moment. He looked almost wild with his thick mass of long, wavy locks—reaching past his shoulders—and full beard. The hair and beard both had an array of colors in it, ranging from light to dark blond, and even a bit of gold. She had guessed right about his size from her vantage point on the ground and now standing, she surmised that he must be somewhere between six foot three or four.

"Whether I am dangerous or not, you shouldn't take my word for it."

Emeline gulped loudly, taking a step back as he took one forward. She saw him reach into his pocket. Fear overtook her once again. "What are you doing?"

The stranger took out his wallet and reached in to grab some bills. "So you can get cleaned up and maybe get some food," he explained while holding the cash out to her.

"What?" She didn't know whether to be offended—she looked down at the holey gray shirt she liked to sleep in as well as her dirt-stained sweatpants—or to admire the kind gesture. She put her hand out in front of her, palm facing him. "Thank you, but I'm good." Embarrassed, and feeling slightly foolish and dejected, she turned away from him and began walking toward her sporty little silver Mazda parked several yards away, and only when she reached the driver's side did she dare turn around. She found him staring at her, and she couldn't help return his gaze for a moment, before finally getting into her car.

"Ugh!" What Emeline saw in her rearview mirror horrified her. Her hair was a complete disheveled mess, with some of it sticking out on the right side, which she had slept on. Smears of dirt stained her cheek, and her eyes were a bit bloodshot with dark circles underneath. She definitely needed to get herself together before her father got a good look at her, not wanting to add to the stress of today. She decided she would pull over a few blocks from the house to change and put some make-up on, but for now, she just needed to get away from here. Without looking back at him, she could still feel the stranger's gaze on her as she drove away.

Several miles later, she still saw his eyes vividly in her mind. They hadn't been judging, but shrewdly assessing, and she had no idea why that brief encounter kept replaying itself over and over. Perhaps because he had seen her at her most vulnerable, unguarded and mourning the loss of what was and could have been. Twenty years later, and the hole inside her soul only got bigger.

****

As she drove to her father's house, Emeline let her mind wander—anything to distract her from images of the stranger's eyes. She hadn't been good at letting people in over the years, but she was working on that, cherishing a few close friendships with some of her coworkers. Relationships, however, were a whole other story. None to speak of in the last two years, and none to write home about before that. Her current *situation* was an unwanted one. What Jarod called a relationship, Emeline called stalking.

They had gone out on two dates after being introduced by a friend of a friend. She figured out that she had nothing in common with him on date one, but he had been charming, giddy even when he told her that they were not only celebrating their first date, but the fact that he had just been made partner at the corporate law firm he worked for. Date number two did not go so well. Jarod had talked mostly about himself, rarely asking

Emeline any questions, and his egocentric colors came out. She was bored and she was done, though she politely sat through the date, grudgingly acquiesced to let him walk her home as he did after their first date, and then firmly declined his offer to invite him upstairs as well as his request for date number three. The texts and calls were only sporadic at first, until they became almost daily and she was forced to change her number. He even had the nerve to invite himself to join her and a few of her coworkers for lunch one day and the gall to call it date number three later. He had pulled up a chair and sat himself down, managing to charm her friends, who were ignorant of the situation at the time.

And who could blame them for their reaction? He was gorgeous, although a little too metrosexual for her taste, especially with his manicured nails, perfectly coiffed black hair, and no five o'clock shadow to speak of. Her tastes leaned towards the more rugged men who never dared wax their eyebrows. Besides caking on the charm, Jarod was also very successful and rich, and probably not a lot of people said no to him, but Emeline did, and as it turned out, he wasn't someone who liked to take no for an answer.

"Just imagine what our children would look like," he had said to her one day when he followed her from the coffee shop to the lobby of her work across the street. "Would you deny them such beauty?"

Perhaps he had thought he was being cute, but Emeline did not. "I'm not having children with you." She had turned to face him, balling her hands into fists. "This is where I work, Jarod. You can't just follow me in here." She pursed her lips and added, "And next time, don't invite yourself over to sit with me and my friends. It's rude!"

She had turned to go, but he grabbed her hand.

"I'll be expecting an invitation soon then." With that, he had left, and she had fumed all the way to her office.

Emeline shook her head, bringing herself back to the present. She pulled her car over next to her childhood home. There would be no dwelling on her *pest* problem today. She put drops in her eyes to clear the redness, concealed her dark circles, and added color to her cheeks, and then after taking out a clean shirt and jeans from her overnight bag, she ducked low to rid herself of her dirty clothes. "I'm going to burn these," she said aloud, remembering the look on the stranger's face as he perused her attire. "Maybe finally invest in some sexy lingerie."

When she deemed herself presentable, she restarted the car and drove another few blocks down to the house her father had bought three years after the death of her mother and brother. Selfishly, she had wished that her father had never sold their home so she could always walk in the footsteps of her happy memories, but unselfishly, it was what was best for him. He didn't need the physical reminders to add to the anguish of the mental ones.

"You are early, *mon ange*," he said to her when she walked into the kitchen to find him drinking coffee and reading the paper.

"*Oui*, Papa, I wanted to get an early start." She tossed her keys on the kitchen counter, and then kissed her father on the top of his head before pouring herself a large cup of coffee. She took a section of his newspaper and joined him at the kitchen table.

They wouldn't talk about what today was, nor would they reminisce about the past. Instead, they'd sit at the kitchen table in companionable silence, drinking their coffees, and then, a short while later, they'd drive over to the cemetery, place flowers on the grave where mother and son were buried together, and then stand there, holding on tightly to one another as they cried silently.

Chapter Two

Emeline was odd. She was probably one of the rarest of people who looked forward to work on Monday mornings, but then again, according to her, that's what happened when you had a job you adored and the first day of the work week signified the start of some exciting new project. This Monday, however, was different, and a sense of dread had filled her from the moment she had woken up.

Publishing Enchanted, where she worked as a Senior Marketing Director, had been her home away from home for the last decade. Once a job she loved, it became a job she feared for, ever since she began to see the publishing company's steady decline in revenue. And then came the announcement from her mentor and boss, Andrea Moore, that she was taking early retirement and selling the company she had built from scratch.

"Is he in yet?" Emeline asked her assistant Christina when she walked into the office.

"I heard he's been in since the crack of dawn," she replied. Christina followed Emeline to her office. "There was one message for you this morning, and I took care of that."

There was no need for Christina to elaborate. Emeline already knew the message had to do with Jarod, and she appreciated her handling him as she had been for the past few months. Though Christina Wagner was normally quiet and a bit shy, she also knew how to be firm. Push her too far, and she bit. Emeline threw her assistant a grateful look and then hung up her sweater on her coatrack. The weather had suddenly shifted this morning, signifying that fall was fast approaching.

"So, what's he like?" Emeline asked her. She sat down at her computer, already powered up for her by

Christina, and entered her password. Several messages were waiting for her.

"Dunno," Christina said. "He hasn't been out of his office yet, but there's a memo."

"Ah!" Emeline noticed said memo in her inbox. "Senior staff meeting at 10 AM," she read aloud. He detailed some key points to be discussed at the meeting and then she couldn't help the laugh that escaped her when she read his sign off. "Sincerely, The New Head Honcho, Adam Charmont."

Christina snorted. "Is that supposed to be a joke?"

"I mean, it would be a great way to break the ice." In truth, Emeline had no idea what to make of this *new head honcho*. She had done her research, or so she thought, when she first began looking into the potential buyer. She learned that Adam Charmont was a master at *hostile* takeovers, and naturally wondered about his interest in simply buying a small publishing company. He had his hands in multiple large corporate investments as well, both in North America and Europe. And on a bit of a personal level, the sixty-seven-year-old was not only known as a philanderer, but he had stopped his charitable donations almost two decades ago, including the charities he had started. *Seems like a swell guy*, Emeline had thought. After hours of poring over the companies he had taken over and mostly dismantled, selling them for parts like a cheap used vehicle, she had hit a bit of a snafu.

Deceased.

Dead men don't buy companies, but Adam Charmont Jr., as it turned out, though he had dropped the suffix, was the actual buyer. This man had inherited an empire, and although he had been crucial in some of his father's earlier dealings, he pretty much went off the grid for a number of years until his father's death eighteen months ago. Instead of resuming Senior's work however,

Junior took a different approach. He flipped dying businesses and turned them into gold before he sold them off for a profit. These businesses were often innovative ventures, rather than just giant conglomerates, but still, they dealt with products and bottom lines, nothing related to art, and the selling off of these companies was a major red flag for her. She wondered what the continuous change of ownership would mean for their little brand and the people who worked hard at maintaining it. Would she still even have a job at the end of this? She may not have had an office on a corner, but it was a nice size, roomy enough for not only her desk and chair, but also for a small couch and a coffee table, and a killer view of Midtown. Along with loving her actual work, and the relationships she had built along the way, her job wasn't something she wanted to easily part with. Skeptical as she was of this new boss, however, she held out hope that he could be the company's saving grace.

Like his father, there were no photographs of Junior Charmont to be found, no social media accounts, but unlike Senior, there was nothing written about his personal life, save for the fact that he was thirty-one years old.

"Knock, knock." DeAnne strolled into her office followed by Rhonda. "Joe just texted, asking if you wanted coffee."

"Hell yeah!" Emeline pumped her fist in the air. "It's pumpkin season." She had no time to stop for coffee this morning and only had the office brew to look forward to until lunchtime. Fortunately, Joe had come to her rescue. "Tell him I'll have a Pumpkin Spice Latte with skim milk, pretty please."

She looked at the faces of her team, thought about Joe across the street, and hoped like hell they would all get to keep their jobs.

"You all right, sweets?" Rhonda asked with motherly concern as was always her way. She had two grown sons and a teenaged daughter at home, and sometimes her motherly affection spilled out on her coworkers.

Emeline was always touched by it. She simply nodded, not wanting to add to the stress of the day with her fears.

"It'll all work out, I'm sure," Rhonda said, though the hesitancy in her voice did not escape Emeline's notice.

An hour and a giant caffeine fix later, Emeline picked up her iPad and headed over to the meeting room. She gave Christina a salute as she passed by her desk. The door was open and the room was empty when she got there. Normally, she'd sit to the right of Andrea, who had sat at the head of the ten-seater, rectangular, mahogany conference table, but for the first time in ten years, she suddenly felt out of place. Making a quick decision, she put her iPad on the table in front of a random seat somewhere in the middle and was just about to sit down when she heard footsteps behind her.

She turned around. *He* stood frozen in the doorway, the stranger from the cemetery, his mouth slightly open and eyes wide in surprise. Quickly, he schooled his features and cleared his throat.

"And you are?" he asked her.

Not a crazy person who likes to sleep in cemeteries. Though she didn't say that. Instead, she cleared her own throat before *actually* answering. "Emeline Bell." *This can't be him*, she thought, but it had to be. He had all the air of a man firmly in charge, despite his uncharacteristic appearance for someone in his position. Notwithstanding the hair and full beard, his attire was all business in what appeared to be an expensive navy blue, pinstriped suit, sans tie. Fortunately, she, too, was appropriately dressed, and no longer a complete mess. Her hair was up and pulled back neatly into a clip with only a few loose strands on the sides, and her ratty shirt was replaced with a crisp, white, feminine button-down, tucked neatly into a charcoal pencil skirt instead of dirt-sodden sweats.

"Adam Charmont," he said, introducing himself gruffly as he finally entered the room and proceeded to the head of the table.

A sly smile formed on Emeline's lips. "The new *head honcho*." She could have sworn his lips twitched as well, but had no time to ponder that since staff members began filing in. Floors scraped as chairs were slid out, and then back in, and all the while she could feel his emerald gaze watching her.

He began the meeting when all the senior staff members were present and seated, wasting no time in getting to the bottom line as soon as he introduced himself. "Sales have been steadily declining for quite some time as I am sure you are all aware, so I have laid out several plans to battle that effect to start with. Change will not happen overnight, but it must happen quickly if this publishing house is going to survive."

Emeline could scarcely look at him, but she listened with rapt attention as his deep, velvety, accented voice resonated throughout the room. And then she did look at him, as anger began to bubble up inside her at some of his intended changes. He talked of quantity, without the mention of quality, and visions of assembly lines began to dance in her head. Price dropping, mass marketing, and outsourcing of cover artists when the demand would be too great on the in-house designers. And then she could no longer hold her tongue when he talked about changes to the logo, or rather the complete redesign of the beloved staple that this publishing house was known for.

"Are you going to change the name of the publishing house as well?" she asked. She didn't bother hiding the sarcastic tone inflected in her question.

"Excuse me?"

"You may as well. The logo has been part of the company since the very beginning," she continued, "and is an identifiable marker of the brand. It's on every book we've published."

"It's outdated," he simply stated, keeping eye contact with her.

She shook her head. The outline of a castle with vines growing all around wasn't outdated in her opinion. It was classic. Upon examining it closely, a set of eyes appeared seemingly hiding amongst the vines, a representation of a secret hidden inside, as there are secrets concealed in the pages of a book. She looked over at her colleague Charlie Jones, the designer of the original logo, and saw her own anger and sadness reflected in his eyes.

Adam Charmont quirked his brow and folded his arms. "You don't agree?"

"I think a complete rebranding may alienate the loyal readers. Just because something is antique doesn't mean it isn't charming. Although," she had a sudden thought that may appease the new boss, as well as actually benefit the logo and brand, "perhaps a bit of revamping, adding some color and maybe a few more elements." She glanced over at Charlie to see a gleam in his eyes this time and knew that the wheels were turning in his head as they were in hers. She shifted her gaze to boss man to find him pensive.

"I'll consider it," he finally said.

A small victory was still a victory, she thought,

and she did actually agree with some of his plans, but perhaps not the way he wanted to go about them exactly. The new website launch, for example, was a great idea especially since that was the area that she had found most lacking. He talked of vendorship, one possibly rivaling the big ones out there. And for someone who stayed away from social media, he had a lot of good ideas and insights on expanding the company's presence on those platforms.

When the meeting ended, he asked Emeline to stay. He waited until everyone else had left before he spoke without preamble. "What were you doing sleeping in a cemetery?" His tone came out much the same as it had the day before yesterday—chastising.

She had been wondering if and when he would bring up their actual first encounter all throughout the meeting, although she had hoped he wouldn't. "I wasn't sleeping in a cemetery. I accidentally fell asleep. And I already heard your lectures on the dangers of it, so can we just move on, please?" Seeing that he was about to ask her something else, she quickly added. "What were *you* doing there?"

The redirection worked. It seemed he did not want to share his personal details either. He furrowed his brows and proceeded to talk to her about her latest projections. He wanted to see something new from her and her team by end of day. Emeline wasn't worried. She had already been cooking something up for a while that she wanted to pitch to Andrea, particularly about expanding genres, and adding new ones, which would by extension increase readership. A whole world of genres and subgenres had been created since the birth of Publishing Enchanted and age ranges had overlapped with many books offering a wider demographic. *This expansion may not be a bad thing,* she thought.

"We're already working on something," she said.
"Good."

She wasn't ready to leave just yet. Not until she got some answers, whether they were owed to her or not. "I have to ask. A publishing company isn't your typical purchase, so why now did you just up and decide to buy a publishing company, and a small one at that? According to my research, you tend to fry fish that are a bit bigger."

He crossed his arms again, an act she was quickly becoming familiar with that he did when being challenged. "A publishing company is a business, no? We sell a product. I bought it to turn it into a *bigger fish*."

"Books aren't your average products, Mr. Charmont. It's not like shampoo for example, where after the bottle is empty it's simply thrown away. A book stays with a reader, or *consumer* as *you* would no doubt put it, for years after they have finished it, perhaps even forever, or at least that should be our goal … to find talent who write books that leave a mark on someone forever."

"Well, *Ms. Bell*, I can certainly see that you are not just a pretty resumé, but you see, the shampoo bottle isn't so different from a book after all. An empty bottle simply means the consumer will buy more shampoo if they love the product, and they will buy other products from the company … lotion, perfume. You get the idea."

"I do," she said, displeased with his comparison, since her intention was to display how much of a comparison it wasn't. And she got it, all right, but *he* apparently still did not. "Books aren't just simple products to consumers, and to the people who work here, this company is more than just a paycheck. We pour our hearts and souls into our work."

He unfolded his arms and leaned forward, placing his palms flat on the table. "Perhaps if you learn to view it more like a business and leave your heart and soul at the door when you come in to work, it wouldn't be going bankrupt."

Her jaw dropped at his words. "End of day," he reiterated, before he pushed off the table and left the meeting room.

Chapter Three

By mid-week, Emeline was dreading going into the office as if all of her previous years of excitement had been sucked out of her. The boss man had liked the idea of expanding and adding genres that she and her team had come up with and planned on implementing them as soon as she got things set in motion with all necessary departments and they presented it to him, but the plans for an assembly-like quality was still on the horizon and she was determined to construct as many charts as she needed to show him that the expansion would generate sales. Instead of outsourcing, promoting from within, and adding on to their in-house staff, as well as continuing to find those diamond in the rough authors, would not only grow the company, revenue included, but would distinguish Publishing Enchanted. She had a feeling however, that no matter how many charts she came up with, no impact would be made. It simply would take longer her way. She put away her sentimentality for a moment, and thought about it from a business standpoint—time really wasn't on their side. The only way to actually preserve the company and keep the revenue going, was to find a way to speed things up.

The art department was given an end of the week deadline. "They have until Friday to impress me," Mr. Head Honcho had said yesterday after deliberating on the revamping of the logo versus changing it altogether. Emeline was going over a mock-up when she heard Christina's clipped tone. She leaned forward to peer out of her doorway and saw her assistant appeared quite angry with whomever she was on the phone with, although Emeline could sense who it was, as usual.

Jarod had apparently decided that this week had not yet been stressful enough for her and upped the number of calls he was making to the office. Too bad she couldn't change the number to the publishing department, every department in it, and make it unlisted.

She called Christina into her office after she ended the call. "Put him through next time, okay?"

"But—"

"Please, Christina. I am going to put an end to this once and for all."

Sure enough, an hour hadn't even passed before he called again. "Hello, Jarod," she said evenly into the phone.

"There now," he drawled, his voice smooth, his tone arrogant. "That wasn't so hard. Meet me for lunch later and—"

Emeline gritted her teeth, losing the cool she tried to keep. "No, Jarod."

"Dinner then. We need to have a conversation, Emeline. Don't be stubborn."

Emeline took in a deep breath to keep from screaming—this had been her way of dealing with stressful situations ever since she was a child. "The only conversation we are going to have is this one. I have had enough of this. Seriously, go fucking find a hobby or something instead of calling someone who wants nothing to do with you." She took another deep breath when she caught her voice rising, but cut him off as soon as he began to speak again. "Because if you don't, Jarod ... if you continue to harass me, I will have you served with a restraining order, very publicly in your office, with your shiny new position. How do you think that will go over?"

She heard him suck in a breath. "You wouldn't? That's our future."

"No, that's your fucking future, which for the hundredth time, I want no part of." Another deep breath. "And I absolutely will if you call me again." She slammed the phone down, shut her eyes for a moment to regain her composure, and when she opened them, her boss was standing in her doorway looking angry.

She wanted to ask him if he often eavesdropped on other people's conversations, or to tell him to suck it if he was about to lecture her on taking personal calls in the office, something she rarely ever did, but she did neither of those things. It wasn't the boss she was angry at … this time. Instead, she calmly inquired, "Did you need something?"

"Charlie emailed me a mock-up. I wanted your thoughts."

His face softened when he stepped inside her office and took the seat opposite her desk. She could only imagine what he was seeing on her face. She felt her cheeks enflamed from anger, but at least her watery eyes were returning to normal. She picked up the paper with the logo on it along with a few of her notes and stared directly at it while she spoke. "I like it, but I think the colors should be more vivid, or different altogether."

"Agreed," he said. "And the extra set of eyes?"

This time she looked up from the paper. "I liked it better when it was just the one set."

He seemed surprised. "Me, too. Makes you wonder why someone or something is all alone."

She nodded. Emeline found herself surprised as well that they could so easily agree on something as well as see the poignancy behind it. "You'd have to enter the castle to find out."

They were silent for a moment after that, until finally he spoke first and told her about bringing in a public relations person he used for his last venture. "We could use a bit more media exposure." He opened his mouth again as if to say something more, but then quickly shut it and stood up. "I look forward to seeing an updated version of the logo," he said before he left.

She was glad he didn't comment. It was the second time he had seen her vulnerable in less than a week, and the last thing she needed was another lecture. She focused on what he had just told her about bringing in a PR person instead and knew it was the answer to speeding things up. The simple buzz about changes, even before they were implemented, could definitely increase sales and even bring back some of their slacking readership.

Melody Bloom, PR extraordinaire, as she referred to herself, arrived the next day with her mousy, brown-nosing assistant in tow. While getting a tour of the office and doing a meet and greet with the staff, Emeline learned that Melody was as fake as her tits, bleached hair, and dragon nails, which she liked to repeatedly tap on various office surfaces. The jury was still undecided about the authenticity of her lips, and by jury, she meant herself, Christina, Rhonda, and DeAnne. Poor Joe was always the odd man out, but then again, he was glad for it.

"If you girls start talking about your damn periods again, I'm eating alone from now on," he groused.

"That's just DeAnne." Emeline rolled her eyes, and DeAnne threw her head back and gave one of her usual devious, raspy laughs.

"Oh please, Joe," DeAnne scoffed. "Your life would be boring without us."

Joe shrugged and gave a noncommittal nod, but of course it was the truth. They had a good camaraderie going, not to mention the fact that they really made a great team and Emeline valued each and every one of them, though they were one team member short now.

Perhaps they were being petty, Emeline thought,

examining Ms. Bloom piece by piece, but the woman walked around with her nose in the air like she owned the place, grating on Emeline's every nerve. Not to mention the fact that she seemed way too chummy and flirtatious with Adam.

When the heck did I start thinking of him as Adam?

What surprised her even more was an unfamiliar emotion that took her a while to place, considering the fact that she couldn't ever recall feeling it—jealousy. And when she noticed that Adam pretty much ignored Melody's advances, even seemed annoyed by it, Emeline felt relief. Almost the same kind of relief she had felt the day before when Adam's assistant Devon finally arrived and turned out to be male, consequently sending Miss Flirty Temp to her next job somewhere else. Devon was someone Adam had pinched from the previous company he had taken over and sold, and he was actually quite nice, fitting in with everyone from day one.

Emeline quickly stomped on her confusing emotions and continued with her work, trying not to cringe every time Melody clapped her hands together and loudly said, "bup bup," when she wanted to get someone's attention. She did have to begrudgingly admit though, after pulling up some information on the Bloom PR firm, that the woman was actually quite good at her job.

On Friday, Emeline sat in on a meeting with Adam and Melody to go over the lines that crossed between marketing and PR. Another range of emotions overtook her when she learned of the charity Adam wanted to start up again. It was one that his father had discontinued long ago—Cancer Families. The charity provided monetary aid, not only for expensive treatments, but to the families facing a financial crisis after the fact, whether their loved ones survived or not.

"Yes, that will definitely bring more attention to the company," Melody said, clapping her hands and then typing away on her laptop. Emeline couldn't help cringing as her nails went clickity clack across the keyboard.

"We have quite a few books that deal with the topic of cancer," Emeline informed them. "Both fiction and non-fiction. We can spotlight them and the authors."

Adam agreed and Melody did as well, though she seemed annoyed, perhaps because the idea hadn't come from her. Another half hour of breathing in Melody's oversaturated perfume, and they finally broke for lunch. A few minutes more, and Emeline's stomach would have embarrassingly made its demands known to the room.

Though she was starving, her mind was hardly on her lunch, but on the meeting she just came from. It only reaffirmed this new mass-produced direction the company was going into. And his words about leaving her heart and soul behind still worried her.

After she got back from lunch, her intercom beeped. "I need to see you in my office, Emeline," Adam said.

Emeline? First, I am calling him Adam in my head and now he decides to call me by my first name. She put her stuff down and then headed over to his office.

"You wanted to see me, *Adam*?" she asked when she entered his office. A spacious room, which *was* located on a corner, and featured a large couch with several accent chairs—a leftover from Andrea. The colors were neutral, making Emeline wonder if he'd even bother renovating the space given the fact that he would more than likely move on soon.

His lips twitched. She could have sworn she saw

the ghost of a smile and suddenly found herself wondering what a full-blown smile would look like on him.

"Have a seat please." He extended his hand toward one of the chairs in front of his desk. "I just want to go over a couple of things with you."

"Okay." Emeline sat down and folded her hands on her lap.

"First, I love the improved logo design. Have you seen it yet?"

"I have," she said. She loved it, too. It stayed true to the original concept, and yet stood out more. She told Adam as much and was glad that they could at least put the notion of a complete redesign to rest.

"And I see that you put in a request to replace Ms. Stevens. Surely you and your team could do without her for a few months while she's on maternity leave. Hiring a temp may be more work than—"

"Daniella actually informed me this week that she will not be returning."

"Oh, why is that?"

"She's decided to stay home full time, at least for a while. She has another little one at home."

Adam's eyes furrowed together, as if he was displeased with something and that made Emeline's insides boil all of a sudden. "Don't tell me you have issues with stay-at-home moms!"

"No, I do not," he snapped, making Emeline feel bad for her accusatory words. "Stay-at-home mothers have one of the hardest, most rewarding jobs out there," he added, making it sound almost personal. "In any case, you and your team have been managing well without her, and again, bringing in a new person may prove more work at this juncture than adjusting without an additional member, therefore I am denying the request."

Before she could add there may have to be some extra-long hours put in, Adam cut in with, "And you and your team will get paid for the overtime, as opposed to paying another salary for someone who in my opinion would prove unnecessary. Should that change in the future, where I see an expansion would be a benefit, we can revisit your request then."

"All right then," she agreed. She'd loved working with Daniella, but he was right that bringing on someone new at this point may not benefit them at all.

"Good, glad that we got that settled, because I actually see this in a few departments, where we have extra people that are doing things that can be done by fewer. One way to increase profit is to, of course, reduce overhead, more so now since I will be bringing on some new players for the website."

Now she really was angry. There was no misreading him this time, and she had already suspected he had cuts in mind. Was he asking her to chime in on this? "Shouldn't this be a matter for you and HR?"

"You oversee many different departments and given your position and acquaintance with staff members, you are the perfect person to determine who might be considered dead weight around here."

"Dead weight?" She took a deep breath to keep from yelling at him. It's not as if she hadn't had a say before in the firing and hiring of candidates, but that was on a case by case basis and only when warranted. This was about him laying good, hard-working people off. "I started here as an intern while I was in college. Andrea took a chance on me, took me under her wing and trained me, and I have known most of these *people* for nearly a decade, all of whom were instrumental in making this publishing house what it is."

"Exactly," he said, raising his voice, but only

slightly. "And what this company would be is bankrupt if I hadn't taken it over."

She hated that he was right—mostly right, anyway. It wouldn't be the first time companies that were underperforming had to make the tough decision of making cuts. However, they had plans for turning things around now. She knew they were close, but not quite there yet where cuts would be necessary right now.

She shook her head. "Well since *you* took it over, then put your big boy pants on and *you* decide who you want to let go."

Adam widened his eyes and leaned back in his chair, folding his arms across his chest along the way.

Damn straight I'm challenging you. "After just a week of you being here, I don't even recognize the company that you want to turn this into and I certainly don't want to be a part of it, or a part of letting valuable people go simply because you feel you need to make cuts to bring in a slew of other people instead of using the talent right under your nose. We still have some time before the in-house cuts would be necessary, but, since you're insistent about getting rid of dead weight, consider this my resignation." She couldn't believe that she actually just said it, but she did and she realized that she absolutely meant it.

He pursed his lips. "If you quit, I'll fire your whole damn team."

"What?" She stood, clenching her fists at her side. "You can't do that. Joe's wife is not working now because she had to take an early maternity leave." She had a dangerous pregnancy, and that hit home for Emeline. "They have two small children. Are you that heartless?" She thought about Rhonda, DeAnne, and Christina and how much this would affect them as well and then couldn't help but wonder how many of the departments she oversaw did his threat extend to.

"Andrea has taught you well," he began, unfazed by her outburst, "but I didn't get good at what I do by not looking at every angle of a situation. And you know what I see?" He didn't wait for her to respond. "I see a very bright and talented Senior Marketing Director who has far surpassed her mentor and has better managing skills. You'll have your own publishing house up and running, and half, if not more, of our authors, investors, and your entire team quitting to come join you. This is business. As I said, you don't think with your heart in business."

"Maybe that's your problem." Emeline felt her blood boiling, but her gaze remained on his, unflinching and adamant in her stance, but he was a bit of a mirror image in his, and as unyielding as she was.

"I haven't had any *problems* flipping dying companies into great success stories and making a huge profit while doing it. I can replace you and your whole team within the week for a bunch of hungry brown-nosers looking to get ahead, and for way less money. But as I said, I believe you to be both a valuable asset as well as a potential future threat to my investment. You may not agree with all of my decisions, but that doesn't make them bad. It makes them ones you don't like. Don't let your anger and pride cost your teammates, your friends, their jobs."

"You're right," she said, but she was about to wipe the smug smile that just appeared, off his face. "I don't agree with your decisions because they aren't innovative, and based on what I've read about you, I expected something more than an assembly line of books. All you do is flip 'em and leave them. You don't stick around to see your work thrive, and I can tell you that there will be no thriving in the long run. Consumers are not going to like your brand of shampoo enough to keep buying more bottles indefinitely." His smugness was replaced with a pursing of his lips and the furrowing of his brows, but he remained silent, which she was glad for because she certainly wasn't done. "I'll admit you're sort of brilliant, so imagine what you could do with this publishing house if you were actually passionate about it, if you wanted to not only make it profitable, but something new and exciting. And you're also right that I can't be responsible for my friends getting fired—" even though she wouldn't be saving everyone's job by staying apparently, "so I guess I have no choice but to stay here." She had one more thing she needed to make very clear. "And for the record, it's not my pride that wanted me to quit. It's because you're an asshole." He looked taken aback by her comment. "And no one should have to work for an asshole."

She didn't wait for a response. She turned her back on his stunned face and left his office, quietly shutting his door behind her.

Chapter Four

Emeline greeted him coolly but professionally when she entered the meeting room on Monday morning. She sat down facing him at the very end of the table. They were both at the head, but today would be her show, at least at the start with regard to the launch of new genres. Adam had his own agenda to share before the end of the meeting and had barely slept all weekend contemplating it.

He suddenly envisioned her team surrounding her when they came in, staring pitchforks at him. He wondered if she had even told them what happened between them on Friday. She had no idea how her words had affected him though. Hell, he was shocked at how *much* they had affected him. He couldn't bring himself to regret his threat, however. He had meant it when he said she was a valuable asset as well as a possible future threat.

Asset. That's exactly what she was, and nothing more, he told himself as he watched Emeline, with her eyes cast downward at her notes. Her lips moved slightly as she read. He looked for nerves and was surprised to find none. Emeline Bell was a pro at her job.

Emeline's assistant Christina entered just then and went directly over to her. "I ... um ... received a response that the ... um ... thing was delivered."

Emeline's gave an almost imperceptible nod. "Thank you." She had replied so quietly to her assistant, Adam had to wonder if he imagined her response. Their cryptic exchange made him curious, although he had a sinking suspicion it had to do with a phone call he had overheard last week. Emeline had been on the verge of tears when she had angrily hung up on a man called Jarod. It sounded as if a disgruntled ex-boyfriend was harassing her, and that made him see red. A real man would have no need to harass a woman.

The shy assistant barely glanced in his direction as she organized the folders on the table, one per seat. She went in and out a few more times to bring in the bagels and then the coffee, setting them in the center of the table. If he had planned the meeting, he would have splurged for something a bit more grandiose. He'd have a talk with his own assistant about that later.

When he and Emeline were alone again, he couldn't help but stare at her as she continued to scan her notes. Her plump, full lips were pressed together. Clearly the message Christina had delivered upset her. It wasn't any of his business, Adam reminded himself, so he didn't ask her questions, despite how badly he wanted to, and despite the sudden urge to tear this Jarod into pieces.

No, he would remain professional and leave her to deal with her own issues. Emeline had haunted him enough since the day he saw her sleeping at the same cemetery where his mother was buried. He had been about to call the police when he saw a prone figure lying on the ground, but then he noticed movement. As he had gotten closer, he had seen that it was a young woman, her face contorted as if experiencing some mental anguish. She had been having a nightmare, it had seemed. A vagabond, a junkie, he had thought at first, but then when she had awoken and faced him with her sharp tongue and eyes full of sadness, it was as if he could see her soul, and he had thought perhaps he had recognized his own tormented one in her. He hadn't even bothered looking at the inscription on the gravestone. Instead, he watched her walk toward her car. Their gazes locked one more time when she turned around, and then she got in her car and drove away. A thought had entered his mind that she may have just been some sort of an apparition, sent to torment him, and yet he feared that he would never see her again, never have the chance to ask what drove her to be there or what had caused her anguish.

To his surprise, his apparition turned out to be none other than the promising dossier he had been reading about when he bought the company.

When Emeline had said those things to him on Friday, it was as if she had held a mirror up to his face and forced him to look at his reflection. He *was* an asshole. Up until that moment, he hadn't even realized it. She'd also complimented him without meaning to, reminding him that he was the one in charge now. Not his father. He could run the company as he saw fit and lose himself in it. And she was right about something else. His plan would be an extreme success, but a short-lived one, before getting lost in a sea of others just like it. He had spent all weekend brainstorming, determined to make this company more than just a monetary success, regardless of whether or not he sold it later.

He was so lost in thought that he had missed it when Emeline looked up from her notes. She caught him staring, but he didn't turn away. Her fine cognac-colored eyes ensnared him. At first glance, she had a quiet beauty about her, with long, straight, caramel hair that could very well have been spun from silk, high cheekbones, clear, fair skin without so much as a blemish to mar it, a small, slightly pointed nose, and full lips. The fact that her bottom lip was a little too full only made her face more interesting, and the longer he examined her features, a realization that hers was one of the most beautiful faces he had ever seen dawned on him.

The spell was broken when other staff members began filing in and then the meeting began. Adam got to see firsthand how well Emeline and her marketing team worked together. Joe Carter, Rhonda Butterbaugh, and

DeAnne Taylor were also staff that he deemed as assets with their impressive knowledge and experience in their field, and he was glad that he didn't have to let them go. A sudden pang of guilt hit him square in the chest at his tactics. He wasn't used to feeling guilty about anything, but suddenly holding Emeline pretty much a prisoner at a job she seemed unhappy in, no doubt because of him, made him feel like all kinds of the putrid stuff one would find at the bottom of a shoe. Still, for all the selfish reasons he did not want to examine, other than the fact that her staying on would benefit the company, he was determined to keep her here, but he was also now determined to make her *want* to stay.

After Emeline and her team had finished their presentation, Adam called Devon in to hand out additional folders, ones that contained a breakdown of his new plan for the company. "I received some good advice recently about longevity." His gaze lingered on Emeline for longer than it should have, but he didn't care. "And I've decided against losing the boutique quality of Publishing Enchanted, but that certainly doesn't mean it can't be a very large boutique." Stunned gasps rang around the room. "With the new press planned and the expansion of genres, I see great possibilities for the influx of revenue, perhaps a bit slower, but with the addition of what else I had in mind..." He gestured toward the blue folders and immediately those seated around the table began to open them. "...even greater in the long run than originally planned."

He was the boss. It was his plan and he was going through with it, yet he looked to Emeline, seeking her approval. When she tore her gaze away from the packet in the folder and he saw the excitement in her eyes, he knew he had gotten it.

They'd start with just one small coffee house/bookstore, featuring only their books and weekly signings by their authors; that and the new website launch would give the company the enormous boost it needed. He had been reading many of the books since before buying the company and had recognized the quality of its authors. He also announced that due to this big undertaking, there would be no layoffs at this time for those who proved they were valuable to the company. No reason not to keep them on their toes, he thought.

He found himself alone again with Emeline after the meeting's end, having purposely stayed behind as she had appeared to do. "You approve of these new changes then?"

She gave him a small smile. "There had been something missing from this company before, some needed push perhaps, and I think you've just found it."

"Maybe I just needed a push."

Emeline nodded and then collected her things. She held up his blue folder. "My team and I will get started on this right away."

Subconsciously, as a way to be near her, he may have timed it that way when they reached the doorway at the same time. He extended his hand out in front of him. "After you." His nostrils flared when he caught the heavenly sent of her herbal shampoo as well as a light, flowery scented perfume or oil. Thoughts of her plum-glossed lips followed him all the way back to his office, and the huge smile currently forming on his face was due to the memory of her praise.

I think you've just found it.

Chapter Five

The week had been full of late nights, and Thursday night was no different. Adam realized that he lost track of time yet again when he glanced at his phone and saw that it was already nearing eight o'clock. He thought he was alone until he heard sniffling sounds outside his office.

"What is it, Emeline? Are you all right?" She was almost to the elevator when he caught up to her, tears streaming down her face.

"I … my…" She could barely speak.

He didn't know what possessed him, but he pulled her to him and hugged her. "Are you hurt?"

She shook her head against him. "N-no." The elevator pinged, and she pulled away from him.

He sprinted for the doors before they closed, and he rode down with her. "Please tell me what happened." His gut was twisting inside seeing her in this state, but at least he was now certain having looked her over that she was in no visible physical pain.

She took a few deep breaths. "My father is in the hospital." She took another few breaths. "His neighbor called. Said he was attacked."

"How bad is it?"

She shook her head as more tears escaped. "I don't know." Her voice cracked on the last word. "I called the hospital, but they had taken him for a CT scan. Some kind of head injury."

His heart broke for her. He knew all too well what it was like to lose a parent. He had lost both of his. "I'll drive you."

She shook her head again. "It's all the way out on Long Island."

"I really don't mind." He'd drive her to the other

side of the country now if she needed. What was an hour and change compared to that?

"If you could maybe just give me a ride home so I could get my car."

"You're in no shape to drive right now," he stated firmly and just then, the elevator door opened to the lobby, but he gently held her back and pressed the floor for the garage. He'd have no argument from her, and she was far too distraught to give him one, it seemed.

"He'll be just fine, I'm sure," he said to her when they got on the road. Not that he knew that for certain, but it was something to say. Perhaps holding on to hope would give her some small comfort.

She stopped crying eventually and just sat quietly for the rest of the drive, facing out of the window and clutching her phone as if it were a lifeline. When they were nearing the hospital, Adam wondered if he should just drop her off, or park and go inside with her, but when they finally got there, he instinctively parked and went with her. If the prognosis about her father wasn't good, he did not want her to be alone.

She seemed in a daze when the automatic doors opened, so he took the lead. He asked her for her father's name.

"Edmund Bell."

Adam gave the information to the security desk, gently coaxed Emeline to give him her ID, and along with his, gave that to the security desk as well. They were fortunately not directed to the ICU, but to a room where they found her father alert and awake.

"Papa!" Emeline practically ran to him and hugged him tight. "Oh, I was so worried, Papa."

She spoke in perfect French. Though Adam's French was far from perfect, and his accent not even close to the flawless one Emeline had, he understood every word. He did recall from reading her resume that she spoke several languages.

"It's just a mild concussion," her father said, also in French, while patting her back. "Don't cry, *mon ange*."

Adam felt like an intruder in their private moment and even a bit envious that he had not had that kind of relationship with his own father, at least not since he was a boy. He was about to step out of the room when her father took notice of him. "And who is this?" he asked.

Emeline sat up and wiped her eyes. "This is my boss, Adam. He was kind enough to give me a ride."

Adam walked the few steps to her father's bedside and shook his hand. "Adam Charmont. Glad to see you are all right, Mr. Bell."

"Please, call me Edmund." He glanced at Emeline before turning his attention back to him. "Thank you for bringing my daughter."

"Who did this to you, Papa?" Emeline cut in, before Adam had the chance to respond. She spoke in English this time.

Not a few minutes later, a police officer entered to inquire about the exact same thing and this time, Adam did step out of the room, but not out of earshot.

"One minute I am working on the fence in my backyard," her father explained, "and the next thing I remember is waking up in the hospital. I didn't see anything."

The next-door neighbor had been the one to find him unconscious and he was the one who called the police. Other than needing a few stitches and being mildly concussed, her father sustained no other injuries and no signs of entry into the house from an intruder was found. This was personal.

"I know exactly who would want to hurt him,"

Emeline burst out saying. "Jarod Folgen." She then uttered "It's all my fault," at the same time the officer asked her why she suspected him. Hearing the name Jarod, Adam immediately knew she was referring to the same man she had been arguing over the phone with last week, but now learning his surname, Adam was surprised that the name was actually familiar to him, and then he recalled why. Jarod Folgen worked in a law firm that he had used before. He had met the man several times, though it was one of the senior partners he had dealt with.

He heard Emeline tell the officer that Folgen had been incessantly calling her and showing up to places where he knew she would be. She'd changed both her cell and house number and on Monday served him with a Cease and Desist order for harassment. She had threatened a very public restraining order, but had a letter delivered quietly by messenger as a warning.

"Do you have any proof?" the officer asked.

There was silence, but then he heard her say, "He did call you a few months ago, Papa."

Her father snorted. When the officer asked what the conversation was about, Edmund told him, "He wanted permission to date my daughter after telling me how fabulous he was. I already knew a little about the shmuck, so I basically told him to fuck off."

Adam couldn't help but smile when he heard Emeline giggle and call her father a "potty mouth". When the officer commented that a phone call made a few months ago was not proof enough, Adam walked in the room. "But you will investigate this man's whereabouts tonight anyway, won't you?"

Officer Fitz, as written on his nameplate, said that he would and that all the neighbors would be interviewed as well to find out if they had seen any suspicious activity.

"Has he ever gotten violent with you before?" Adam asked Emeline.

"No, but Christina told me he sounded very angry when he called on Monday." She paused, thoughtful for a moment. "He has always been persistent and beyond annoying, but I never thought him capable of this."

"And you're sure this was his doing?" her father asked her.

"I don't know, Papa. I don't know what he has to gain by this."

"Certainly not your favor," Adam remarked. "Revenge maybe."

"Why not just come after me then?"

"Hey!" Edmund took his daughter's hand. "I'm glad it wasn't you, *mon ange*."

They sat together like that for a little while longer, with Adam lurking awkwardly and occasionally making small talk. "Charmont? Is that French?" her father asked him at one point.

"On my great-grandfather's side, but we mostly hail from England." Edmund seemed pleased that he understood and spoke French, though Adam continued speaking in English even when father and daughter switched to French. He told them about his dual citizenship since he was born in the US due to his father relocating here for a while. He left out the part that he moved to England at age twelve right after his mother died. His father wanted as little reminder as possible that the woman he loved was gone.

And finally, when Adam was about to excuse himself to give them some privacy, not knowing if he should continue to stay, Edmund told Emeline to go home and get some rest. At her protest, he said, "I will be sleeping and monitored all night. There is no point for you to be here."

He gave Adam a pleading look. "Will you take her home, please?"

Emeline finally acquiesced after Adam promised her the day off tomorrow so she could come back and be with her father. Meanwhile, he'd be doing some investigating on a certain Mr. Folgen and getting more security for the office building.

She didn't say much on the way to and in the car. In fact, she looked downright exhausted and ended up falling asleep not fifteen minutes into their drive. He had already asked for her address and decided to let her sleep until they pulled up to her apartment building.

At one point during the hour-long drive, however, he thought about pulling over so that he could wake her when he glanced over at her and noticed her making that same face she had when he had seen her at the cemetery. She moaned a few times as if she were in pain and then he heard her whisper, "We should be four."

Not for the first time that night, he had no idea what possessed him, but he reached over and took her hand in his, hoping that maybe it would bring her some comfort to know she was not alone. She stopped whimpering then, and her face became peaceful. He continued to hold her hand until he pulled up to her apartment building. She awoke when he gently shook her shoulder, seemingly disoriented at first, and then he got out of the car and went around to her side to open the door.

"I'll see you to your elevator," he said firmly. He was a gentleman, after all, which was also why he did not say he would walk her to her apartment. Her image may no longer be haunting him now that he got to see her again and on a regular basis, to know her a little, but she was doing other things to him, to his libido, which up until he met her, had been occasionally quenched, but bored at best. Still, he would not be sainted anytime soon.

He was satisfied to see that her building had a doorman and security cameras and when the elevator arrived he said, "I'll see you Monday. Try and get some sleep."

"Thank you, Adam." It seemed as if she wanted to say more, but after not saying anything else for a beat, she turned and got into the elevator, her gaze remaining firmly on him until the doors closed.

"Shit," he muttered when he got back into his car. He was definitely in trouble.

Chapter Six

The police hadn't been able to come up with any leads over the weekend. Jarod had been out with a group of people that night, though Emeline thought he still could have done it since they did not know the exact length of time her father had been unconscious. Given his reputation at a prestigious law firm, Emeline was sure that played a part in his no longer being a suspect. The bastard even had the nerve to send flowers to the office on Monday with a card that read, "Hope your father is doing well," and he signed it, "Yours, Jarod". She asked Christina to toss them, but not before Adam had seen them. He walked over to her and boldly took the card out of Christina's hand.

"Just going to go get rid of these," Christina said, and then she scurried off.

"I think maybe you should look into that restraining order," Adam said. He gestured for her to go into her office, and she agreed. Better to have this conversation in private. He ripped the little notecard to pieces before tossing it into her trashcan, and then he closed the door.

"If he continues to call me, I will, but he hasn't since he received the Cease and Desist letter last week." Adam was about to protest that he had made contact by sending her flowers, but she had to point out that he was contacted by the police this weekend and if he was in fact innocent of the attack on her father, the flowers could have been another attempt to get into her good graces. Flowers and a get-well note would hardly be proof to obtain a restraining order. If he had sent dead roses and maggots with a note that read "I'll kill you," that would have been another story.

Her answer seemed to appease him for the

moment, and she found herself genuinely touched by his concern as well as for how he had been there for her on Thursday. He had even texted her over the weekend to ask about her father. Who knew that underneath that tough as nails exterior there was a man with such a kind heart?

"If he does contact you again, you'll let me know?"

She was about to answer yes, but this was too much that he was trying to do for her. He was her boss, and what was going on between her and Jarod was her personal life. "Adam, I really appreciate everything you've done, but I can handle it."

He seemed unhappy with her answer, and then he gave her a curt nod and left her office. Emeline slumped down in her chair when he closed the door behind him. She only hoped she did not offend him in any way, but she was dangerously close to having feelings for this man. She had to push away the rightness of him being with her on Thursday. Her father had said nothing, but in his eyes she saw approval. Adam Charmont was a gentleman and she may have just been dreaming, but she could have sworn that he had held her hand at some point on the drive home. Whether he did or it was only imagined, she had liked the way it felt a little too much.

It didn't matter. He was her boss. And only a little over a week ago, she could barely tolerate him, even though she could not deny the instant physical attraction. She was scared of him at first, being that she was alone with a strange behemoth of a man after waking up from one of her recurring nightmares in a cemetery, not another soul in sight, but she had also felt drawn to him on some level. The memory of his striking eyes had remained with her until she saw them again in person.

A little before lunchtime, she thought about going

to his office to talk to him, but to say what really, she had no clue. It was either let him in or keep him out and remain professional. Although, the more she thought about it, it had entered her mind that they could simply be friends. She was, after all, friends with her team, and hung out with them outside of work. There was no reason to brush him off as she did simply because of a few pesky butterflies that she was determined to shoo away, but at the same time, she'd stick to taking care of the Jarod situation on her own. There was no way she'd run to Adam like some damsel in distress if and when the bastard contacted her again. She had resources for that, the law for one, mace and a whistle in her purse for another.

But perhaps lunch would be a nice gesture. His assistant usually ordered lunch for him which he ate in his office alone. He'd made a change, one that got everyone excited again, therefore it would be nice to include him in something as simple as a group lunch.

She'd made up her mind, squared her shoulders, walked over to his office, and knocked on the door.

"Come in," she heard him say.

When she opened it, he wasn't alone. Sitting across from him was a gorgeous, raven-haired woman with legs that went on for miles. She wore a sleeveless mock turtleneck with a short, cream-colored pleated skirt. A long gray sweater was draped on the back of her chair. Though her outfit may have been a bit scant, it was still quite classy. She wasn't overly made up, a natural beauty, and the perfumed scent she wore made Emeline want to ask her the name of it so that she could go out and buy it.

No introduction was needed, for Emeline anyway, since she knew exactly who the woman was, but Adam gave it anyway. "Emeline Bell, meet Sabine

Shaw." He gave no indication who the famous lingerie model was to him.

Emeline said hello, smiled politely, and refrained from asking her the brand and exact shade name of the lipstick she was wearing, nor did she tell her that she had almost purchased the sexy little red baby doll nightie last week that she had been modeling. Instead, Emeline told her little green-eyed intruding monster to go crawl back into whatever hole it scurried out from, and wither away. She did *not* do the whole jealousy thing.

Sabine, meanwhile, barely even glanced at Emeline. She may as well have been invisible.

"Did you need something, Emeline?" Adam asked her, snapping her out of her inner confrontation.

Yes, I wanted to ask you to lunch so you wouldn't have to eat alone. "Just to go over something with you, but it can wait."

"Brilliant," Sabine said in her lilting English accent. "Now you can hurry up and take me to lunch."

Once again Emeline smiled politely. *Guess he won't be eating alone today after all.* "Enjoy your lunch," she said to the both of them before excusing herself. She'd have to come up with something to go over with him when he returned and no time like the present.

She hurried over to Rhonda's desk and sat herself down on the corner of the table. They went over some ideas, or rather re-went over them, and even though Rhonda seemed a bit confused as to why they were having a similar conversation to the one they had had an hour ago, she went along with it.

The door to Adam's office opened. Sabine walked out first wearing a huge smile on her face, Adam following behind. DeAnne walked over to her and Rhonda. "Holy shit! That's Sabine."

"Who is Sabine?" Joe asked, but when he followed DeAnne's gaze, his jaw dropped open.

"Wife has a lot of catalogues lying around, does she?" DeAnne laughed wickedly at him. She said something else, but Emeline wasn't paying attention. She was staring at Adam by the elevators with Sabine, locked in easy conversation. When they had disappeared through the elevator doors, only then did Emeline turn around. Joe was no longer near them, but at his desk on the phone. Christina, however, was standing beside her.

DeAnne gave her a peculiar look. "You didn't hear a word I just said, did you?"

"Er ... sorry, no."

"Oh. My. God." DeAnne plopped down in the chair in front of Rhonda's desk. "You like him."

"I do not," Emeline replied adamantly, maybe a bit *too* adamantly.

"You were looking at him all moony eyed." DeAnne paused with an odd look on her face. "Come to think of it, I've never seen you look at anyone like that, but it's what I imagine moony would look like on you."

Rhonda shrugged while Christina nodded and then Joe walked over and began nodding, too. "What are we nodding about?"

Emeline rolled her eyes and huffed. She got up and started to walk toward the elevators. "Are you buttinskis coming or am I eating alone today?"

Emeline refused to talk to her team on the elevator ride, and continued with the silent treatment the entire half block it took them to get over to the deli. She also refused to acknowledge their snickering and Joe's constant pleas to be filled in on the "joke".

After they ordered their food and sat down, Emeline decided to end the silent treatment. "I do not like him." She then took a healthy bite out of her turkey club, after which she looked pointedly at the girls and a confused looking Joe for good measure, daring any one of them to challenge her. Of course, they broke out in hysterical laughter, Joe included. He gifted her with an unpleasant view of the contents in his mouth in the process. Emeline simply rolled her eyes again and took another bite. With her mouth still full, she mumbled. "Well, I am certainly not blind." His face was somewhat of a masterpiece, a combination of boyish, rugged, and handsome without being too pretty. Unlike another guy she knew who probably looked in the mirror daily and told himself how beautiful he was. "Thinking that someone is good looking does not equate to having feelings for them."

"Who said anything about feelings?" DeAnne put down her sandwich and raised an eyebrow.

Damn it!

"Come on! That's enough teasing the poor girl," Rhonda chided.

"Don't tell me you have the hots for the new boss?" Realization finally dawned on Joe, but before Emeline had the chance to rebuff his statement, he jerked and yelped. One of the girls must have kicked him under the table. "What? The guy wanted to turn us all into corporate drones. You said so yourself, Emeline."

"Maybe at first," Christina said. "But with the way the company was going ... at least we will still have jobs in a year."

"He does have a great new plan for the company, I have to admit," Rhonda added. "And what about what he did for Emeline last week?" She gave Emeline's hand a squeeze.

Her team knew what had happened to her father and how Adam had driven her all the way out to Long Island and stayed with her. She had called Christina on

Friday from her father's house to let her know she wouldn't be coming in and filled her in on the why. And then Rhonda, DeAnne, and Joe had all called throughout the day, as well as Christina, to check on her and her dad. What she didn't tell them was that Adam was holding their jobs over her head. She knew that they wouldn't let her stay stuck in this position because of them, not even Joe, who it would probably affect the most financially. She'd made her choice, and Rhonda was right. This new direction made the job feel exciting again.

A part of her was still angry that he'd basically held her hostage at the company, but she had to admit that it was also good business on his part. Emeline *would have* eventually taken a slew of clients with her. And then when her company was up and running, most of, if not all, of her team would have joined her, taking a whole bunch of new company secrets with them. And it had been getting harder and harder to truly stay angry at a man, who for no reason whatsoever, went out of his way for her last week. She found compassion, where at first she thought he had none.

"Hello … Earth to Emeline." DeAnne waved a hand in front of her. "Where'd you go just now?"

"Nowhere." Emeline took another big bite of her sandwich. "He's the boss for heaven's sake. Since when does that ever work out well? And secondly, I'm really not his type, anyway." Images of him and the gorgeous supermodel came to mind, along with the easy way they had interacted with each other. She wondered if they were a couple, and the thought of that being the case made her stomach churn.

"Oh honey, you're everyone's type," Rhonda said. "Have you looked in the mirror?"

Joe winked. "I'd date you if I wasn't married."

Emeline scrunched up her nose. He was a

harmless flirt and way too sweet. "No, you'd be running after Jenna like a lost little puppy dog and begging her to marry you." It was easy to see how much he was in love with his wife on the many occasions that Emeline had hung out with them.

"Fine, but you'd definitely be my second choice."

Emeline snorted. "Great! What every girl wants … to be someone's number two." She envied Joe. He had an adorable, kind-hearted wife, and they were soon to be parents for the third time. "But maybe I'll get lucky one day like you and Rhonda and find the kind of love you both did." She turned to DeAnne. "You get way too lucky." Emeline dodged a flying potato chip before turning to Christina. "And you're too sweet not to get lucky soon."

"She *needs* to get lucky soon," DeAnne added, only she wasn't fast enough to dodge Christina's chips.

The subject of love lives, or lack thereof, was fortunately changed after that and they were able to finish their lunch without any more flying potato chips.

Sometime after lunch, Adam knocked on her open door. "You had something to go over with me?"

Shit! She completely forgot about that. "Erm … no, never mind. Still working on it."

Adam lingered in her doorway. "Everything all right?"

She gave him a small smile. "I'm fine."

She was not fine though. How could she be when she could not deny the fact that she was developing feelings for her boss, who may or may not be dating a supermodel, regardless of which, he was still her boss, someone she butted heads with, someone she had called an asshole and completely meant it at the time. Her work was her sanctuary, threatened briefly, but springing to life again. She didn't want some fling to end in disaster, and if she was being completely honest with herself, she felt terrified at the possibility of finding the kind of relationship that *didn't* end in disaster. She had seen what true love looked like, and what the loss of it did to someone.

Even her butterflies now fluttered in disappointment.

Chapter Seven

"Where do you go when you're all spaced out like that, Adam?" Sabine asked, snapping her fingers in front of his face. He hated when she did that.

"Nowhere," he lied. He was thinking of Emeline … again. He had been furious when he saw the flowers that morning, his gut telling him they were from Folgen. It was bad enough that he had felt twisted up inside all weekend thinking that the vicious attack on her father had been calculated as some sort of revenge against Emeline. The woman had bite to her, no doubt, but she was good, kind-hearted, and fucking kept a job to spare her coworkers from losing theirs. This was not a person who lied, cheated, and manipulated to get what she wanted, unlike Folgen, and it made his skin boil to think of that snake causing her pain.

Adam had done some digging over the weekend, having retained his father's contacts in the police department. Other than a few parking tickets, and an arrest for public indecency for having sex at night on a park bench—which got thrown out—Jarod's record was clean. He was known to fight dirty and win big cases for large corporations, making it easy to see why he was promoted. It frustrated Adam that there was nothing concrete he could use against him. Instead, he hoped his threat had done the trick.

Emeline had said she could handle it on her own. Adam had no doubt of that. He got the impression that she handled way too much on her own though, so whether or not she wanted his help, she was getting it. It stung a little that she didn't. Then again, he only had himself to blame for that, given the way he had acted toward her.

And when she had stopped by his office earlier,

he thought he saw a flash of disappointment in her eyes when she found Sabine sitting there, but maybe that was just wishful thinking on his part. He hadn't cared for the way the woman currently seated next to him at his dining table, sipping his expensive red wine, had barely given Emeline a second glance, as if she were not even worth her time to have a simple conversation with.

Sabine was beautiful no doubt, charming even, and they had kept each other's beds warm on and off again when it suited them. There was no love, but a mutual understanding that for one, Adam wasn't interested in the girlfriend thing, and for another, Sabine was focused on her career and all the men she got to date because of it, though there were times he thought perhaps she wanted more from him.

He hadn't seen her in almost a year until earlier today when she showed up at his office. Adam hated having his photo taken, especially by people who would use it for nothing other than gossip mongering, therefore he had insisted on a small, quiet restaurant for lunch, with a table in a corner in the back, and when Sabine had pouted and asked to have dinner with him as well, he would only agree if it were in his apartment. She didn't seem to mind.

Sabine put her wine glass down and stood, smiling seductively at him. Then she sat down on his lap and put her arms around him right before she kissed him. Just a meeting of lips that lingered together at first and then her tongue invaded his mouth, her hand traveling down his chest to his stomach, down to his... "What's the matter?"

He stood abruptly, disentangling her in the process and setting her on her feet in front of him. Nothing. Not even a small twitch from her touches. In fact, he felt a bit repulsed, and it startled him how much he wanted her taste out of his mouth. He took a large swig of his wine.

Sabine looked disappointed. "Maybe you are just too full," she suggested.

"Maybe." He didn't want to insult her, but filling his bed with her tonight would only make his void seem bigger. It wasn't her touch, taste, or her smile he craved. He thought of a pair of haunting cognac eyes and supple lips and suddenly Sabine's smile grew wide again.

"There now. I think he's ready."

She reached for him, but this time Adam caught her wrist before she could make contact. "This isn't happening tonight, Sabine. I'm sorry."

She stepped back, her eyes widening. "You've met someone." It wasn't a question, more like an accusation, but Adam neither denied or confirmed it. "And you have feelings for her?"

Adam ran his hands through his hair, pulling it back away from his face. "Look, I have a lot going on right now with work."

Sabine stepped closer to him again and put her hand on his chest. She seemed pleased when he held it, but she misunderstood his intent. It was to keep her from roaming again. "You're obviously not with her if you're here with me instead, and I know you don't like complications in your life, Adam. You and I are simple. I can make you forget her."

He didn't want to forget her, not when he couldn't remember the last time he actually felt excited about getting up in the morning, or the last time he thought about a woman's smile, the smell of her hair, or anything at all for that matter when she wasn't in his presence. And Sabine just being in his company right now, with her hand on him, only made him think of Emeline more, wishing that she was in Sabine's place.

Adam let go of her hand and moved away from her, far enough so that she couldn't touch him again without him being able to sidestep her right away. "I really need to get some work done. I have an early day tomorrow. Come." This time he held his hand out to her. "I'll drive you to your hotel." He wasn't a complete bastard, after all. The least he could do was drive her, rather than just call her a cab or let her fend entirely for herself.

She glared at him, downed the rest of her wine, then brushed past him, slapping his hand away in the process. He followed her out of his apartment. When they were in the elevator, she folded her arms across her chest and stood there petulantly, with her back turned to him. Finally, when they were in the car, she spoke. "When you're done moping, you know where I'll be. And being the mature adult that I am, I will still consider attending your charity ball."

He wanted to tell her not to bother, but instead, he thanked her, not that he had invited her in the first place. He had simply told her about the charity ball, as well as a work function he was planning to build up the company morale, while they ate dinner as general conversation. He had left out the part that he had been responsible for the loss of morale in the first place, as well as how near and dear the charity was to his heart. He and Sabine had only ever had surface level conversations, nothing deep. She had squealed and clapped her hands together frantically, stating how much she loved a good ball. Then immediately, Sabine started talking about a dress she would have made for her for the event.

Ever the gentleman, as his mother had instilled in him, Adam walked Sabine to the lobby, gave her a kiss goodnight on the cheek, and hoped like hell that she got the message that their physical relationship was over.

He saw Emeline's eyes behind his own lids before he fell asleep that night.

****

"I cannot believe you are dating Sabine Shaw," Melody shrieked through the phone.

"We are not dating." Adam's voice, on the other hand, was monotone. He cursed the photographer who managed to snap a photo of him and Sabine in the lobby. "Sabine's New Boy Toy," they fucking labeled it, though the photo only showed him in profile, placing a kiss on Sabine's cheek, and even that was partially obscured by his hair and fortunately, his name was nowhere to be found. Still, everyone at work had seen her with him on Monday and no doubt knew it was him if they had the chance to look at a rag, which, by the extra-long stares he had been on the receiving end of these past few days, no doubt some of them had.

Sabine knew better than to give his name out. Now he just needed to make it clear to Melody. "There better not be one fucking thing even hinting that it's me in the photo, Melody. Are we clear?"

For the first time since knowing her, a silence stretched before she spoke. "Yes, of course, Adam. I work for *you*."

Damn right! He almost felt bad about being a bit gruff with her … almost. Not a few seconds later, she opened her mouth again.

"But you can't deny the publicity it would bring to the company. Now, we don't have to acknowledge that it was you in the photograph of course, or imply a romantic connection, but you said she was already attending the charity ball, why not have her at the race?"

"Triathlon, Melody." Adam rubbed his temple with his free hand.

"Er … right. Think about it. Not only paid press,

but free press, all talking about the new and improved Publishing Enchanted. A super model, who loves the books, coming out to join in a little office fun."

He had to admit that Melody had a good point. "Fine, I'll talk to her."

"Ooh, and I could totally see you in a man bun. I can already picture all the swooning and panty dropping when you give your interview."

"We discussed this already, Melody." Now he was getting pissed. "I don't do interviews. You are the Public Relations person, so it's your job to relate to the fucking public. Are we clear?" He hated interviews almost as much as he hated to be photographed. What were photographs but reminders of a past you couldn't get back? They were taunting as well as displays served up for scrutiny. Interviews, well, they tended to focus on personal life more than business, and Adam's personal life was not one he wished to share.

"So testy today." She gave him one of her fake laughs. "As you wish. We'll talk over lunch on Friday."

He ended the call just as a knock came at his door. "What?" he practically roared.

Emeline opened the door, but hovered in the doorway. "You wanted to see me?"

He wanted to see her every day. She, on the other hand, had been mostly avoiding him this week. "Yes. That report I asked you for?"

Emeline placed a hand on her hip. "It's on your desk. Christina brought it over to you thirty minutes ago."

He looked down on his desk and sure enough, there it was. His head snapped up, and he pierced her with an angry glare. "Why didn't *you* bring it to me?"

"I wasn't aware that was a requirement for the report," she replied, her tone haughty. "If you needed to see me along with it, next time specify that."

Silence stretched between them as they both glared. It was as if they were having a staring contest and neither wanted to lose. Emeline, however, spoke first but her eye contact remained.

"Was there anything else?"

Adam sighed, wishing he didn't have to feel like a fucking pariah around her. He wanted her to let him in, to know her. More importantly, he wanted her smiles, rather than her unflinching, disdainful glare. Although, he could not expect that of her, not when he wasn't sure he could actually give her anything of himself. What surprised him the most was that he actually found himself wanting to.

"Emeline..." He wanted to apologize for snapping at her, wanted to ask if she saw the photo, if it bothered her enough to keep her distance. But he didn't. "No, nothing else."

He managed to make some peace between them by end of day when he expressed how pleased he was with the report, and he hoped she would be excited tomorrow when he announced what he had planned after he ironed it all out with Melody at lunch. He himself was excited. And when he saw Emeline go into a coffee shop across the street from work on Friday morning, he decided to fill her in. He would not subject her to Melody's company at lunch, however, especially given that Sabine would be there as well.

He crossed the street, a small smile forming on his face, a smile that quickly died when he saw her having a heated discussion with Folgen over by the sugar and milk station.

"Sorry to have kept you waiting," he told Emeline as soon as he reached her. Despite her look of confusion, she did not contradict him, nor did she protest when he took her hand, entwined it with his, and positioned himself slightly in front of her.

"I actually just got here," she replied softly.

Folgen's face contorted to one of rage. "Don't tell me you're fucking *him*, Emeline." His voice carried, causing unwanted stares in their direction.

Adam stepped closer to him, never once letting go of Emeline's hand. "Watch your fucking mouth, or I *will* do as I promised." His voice was low and menacing.

"I don't respond well to threats," Folgen said, but Adam did not miss the flinch on the man's face when he had stepped toward him.

"And I don't respond well to someone harassing my girl. I have far more reach than you, Folgen. Remember that."

He tugged on Emeline's hand gently and walked out of the coffee shop. "I'll get Devon to run out and get you something," he told her as they crossed the street. He still kept her hand tucked firmly in his.

When they entered the lobby, she pulled her hand away. "You threatened him?"

"His job. Yes. I know the senior partners at his firm quite well, actually." She widened her eyes and was about to speak, but quickly he added, "I don't need one of my staff harassed at work. It's bad for business."

He knew he shouldn't have said that the moment it came out of his mouth. She flinched as if he had just slapped her.

"Your staff, huh? A minute ago, he thought I was your girlfriend." She turned from him and headed for the elevators.

As they stood side by side, waiting for the lift to arrive, he wondered if that would be such a bad thing … for her to actually be his girlfriend. He'd never really had one before, since none of his relationships had ever been long term.

The doors opened, and they stepped inside, moving to the back to allow the other passengers to come in. "Won't your actual girlfriend mind?" she whispered to him.

He dipped his head down to whisper in her ear. "She's not my girlfriend." A small, satisfied smile played on his lips when she gazed up at him. Emeline frowned in response, and he wanted to know what was going on in her head. "Don't believe everything you read, Emeline. Tabloids contain more fiction than our books."

She nodded. "You didn't have to do that, but I appreciate it."

"Well, maybe now he will back off." He doubted it, and the look on Emeline's face said she did as well. At the very least, he'd know that now she has some back up.

He did not allow Emeline to protest his offer for sending Devon to get coffee. He insisted, and she stubbornly acquiesced, while he discovered her weakness for all things pumpkin flavored.

Later, he had the lunch from hell, sitting with two women, both not only competing for dominance, but also for his attention. Melody may have been excited on the publicity side of things for Sabine's presence, but she also seemed interested in Adam, an interest he did not share. The female version of a pissing contest was far different than a male's. Men don't attempt to hide their dislike with fake smiles, and insults delivered in the form of compliments. They beat their chests, and boast about size, while these two just feigned becoming the best of friends.

Despite all that, they somehow managed to iron out the details for both events. The venue for the ball was set for the first weekend in December, and the license for the park in Northern New Jersey was already in the works with the space for the triathlon booked for two weeks from tomorrow. Now all he had to do was announce it to his staff.

He called an entire staff meeting in the hub of the office. He hated being the center of attention, but seeing the curious faces of the staff, especially Emeline's, encouraged him. He started with the charity ball. "Attendance is by no means mandatory, but since Publishing Enchanted is the sponsor, it would be greatly appreciated, not only in support of the company, but for this amazing charity as well. Every employee member is entitled to two tickets for the ball." He hadn't been seeking approval, not for something that would help at least a part of his soul to heal, but it seemed he got it anyway. He saw heads nodding, whispers of how wonderful the cause was when he explained it in detail, and he knew then that most if not all of them would come to show their support.

"We also have some new faces here with us, and I hope you all welcome them into the fold," he went on. He'd kept his word about not firing anyone, but he did need the additional hires for the new website, deciding it was best to keep everything in-house.

"And finally, I know there has been quite a bit of tension with the change of ownership, but I do hope that we are all past that at this point. I see great things for Publishing Enchanted, groundbreaking and innovative, and I would like to rebuild the sense of community here that I know from Andrea you've all had before. Therefore, we are going to host a triathlon, two weeks from tomorrow for employees and their families. You'll receive an email with all the details next week. Now, I know it's October, and the water isn't exactly swim friendly, so we will replace that portion with row boats on the lake. It's all in good fun, but there is nothing wrong with a bit of competiveness every now and then, so you can pair off, form teams, or go at it solo if you wish, and the winning team or individual, first one to reach the end, will get two extra paid days off."

Melody stepped out of the crowd to join him, and give some detail about the publicity of the event. He searched Emeline's face, hoping to see some excitement there, but there was none. She seemed upset, while an excited buzz went around the room, including from her direct team. Joe had even been talking about forming an alliance since his wife and small children would not be able to compete, and DeAnne, Christina, and Emeline were single. He goaded Rhonda about them kicking her and her family's butts.

"Bup, bup." Melody clapped her hands together. "And even more exciting news, we will have a celebrity there to celebrate with us. If you haven't heard of Sabine Shaw, then you have been living under a rock. She has graciously agreed as a personal favor to me—" Adam wanted to snort, "to take part in the competition. She'll be pairing up with our own Adam here. Now, he will be ineligible for the prize, but..." she gave Adam a wink. "Well, you may all just have to strive for second place."

After the announcement, the vibe around the office was exactly what he had hoped for. everyone lingered, speaking excitedly not just to each other, but to him as well. Everyone but Emeline. She had quietly left the hub and walked into her office, closing the door behind her.

Chapter Eight

Emeline and Adam were the last ones to stay again. She knew he was still in because his door to his office was slightly ajar with the light still on. She decided to tell him now that she would not be attending the triathlon.

"And why not? Surely you haven't got something that you can't maybe postpone for another weekend?"

She had no other plans, but he did not need to know that. "You can't just expect people to drop what they're doing at such short notice," she said stubbornly. "You did say that attendance wasn't mandatory."

"You're my head of marketing. You should be there. Your entire team is going to be there from what I gathered." He crossed his arms looking displeased, and then he uncrossed them and stood, placing his palms flat on his desk. "This isn't because of Sabine, is it?"

"What?"

"You're not jealous, are you?"

How dare he assume that? She may well have been jealous, battling unfamiliar feelings, ones that she had already acknowledged to herself she had not felt for anyone before, but he stood arrogantly in front her, practically demanding she reveal herself to him and for what? His ego? No way would she do that.

She matched his smug smile with a saccharine one of her own and walked over to his desk. She then mimicked his stance and put her hands on the table. "I know you're probably used to getting any woman you want. I mean look at you … handsome, rich, intelligent, hell, I'd be lying if I didn't say I thought about taking you for spin." She knew she was out of line, but she continued. "Is that what this whole triathlon is about? Buttering people up, getting them to like you, getting *me* to like you? That's probably what you're used to, isn't it? Money and looks can only get you attention, though. You can't pay people to actually like you."

"Get out of my office," he said quietly, his face a mix of anger and hurt.

He may have been an asshole to her, but he was never intentionally cruel, like she had just been, and she felt ashamed for it, instantly regretting her vile words, especially when he was really not the cause of her upset.

"Adam, I—"

"I said get out!" This time he yelled the words.

She practically ran out of his office, swiping at the angry tears pouring down her cheeks. Her anger was directed solely at herself. She frantically pressed the call button for the elevator and was thankful that she didn't have to wait long. At least she had a long drive to her father's house to calm down, even if she had to break down in the car to do it.

The parking garage was eerily quiet, and when she looked down at her watch to see that it was after eight, she understood why. She let out a sigh of relief when she saw a security guard sitting in the booth, but her anxiety picked up a bit when she went around the bend and he was out of sight. There were security cameras everywhere, so she tried not to panic.

Another sigh of relief escaped her when she finally reached her car. She made a mental note to have her keys out and ready next time so she wouldn't have to fumble in her bag trying to locate them. Finally, she found them, but the slam of a car door behind her made her turn around sharply and drop them.

Three men were walking toward her, one of them looking her up and down and leering. They were young, early twenties she surmised, dressed in casual jeans and t-shirts that looked as if they needed a good wash. All three wore baseball caps. She fumbled in her purse again, trying to locate her mace and whistle, and cursed the fact that tasers were illegal in New York.

She didn't find either mace or whistle in time. One of them had grabbed her bag and threw it on the ground.

"Just take it," she said, referring to the purse.

One of them pulled her toward him and spun her around so that her back was against his front. He held one of her hands painfully behind her back and the other at her throat. "Your bag isn't what we want."

The third guy, the one who leered at her, his cold, dark eyes sent shivers down her spine. No, her purse wasn't what they wanted at all. He stepped closer to her and tilted up her chin. "That's a pretty shirt you're wearing. Why don't we see what's underneath?" He pushed her open sweater jacket down one of her shoulders and then slid his pointer finger down her chest along the path of the buttons on her blouse.

Emeline felt herself shaking, her fear of what they were about to do to her nearly choking her, but she was determined not to go down without a fight. She slammed her foot down hard on the foot of the guy holding her and pushed against the two men in front. Their momentary shock gave her the momentum to break free and run, but her freedom was short-lived. One of them grabbed her by the back of her sweater, yanking her back, and then he fisted her hair with his free hand and pulled hard. She screamed.

"That hurt, you little bitch," he said as he brought her back flush against his body. She wanted to vomit from the feel of his hot breath against her ear, and then a second later, he was gone, as if ripped away. She spun to see him flying backwards against a car and then Adam slammed his fist into the jaw of the man who'd leered at her. The one who dropped her purse received a hard kick to the ribs. Meanwhile, she stood frozen in place, shivering, all the while Adam, with ferocity and skill, beat them. She saw blood spatter on the floor, and the owner of the blood had his nose gushing. Then came the agonizing sound of pain when an arm was twisted, more than likely hard enough to break a bone, and only when she saw a flash of metal was she able to utter a sound. Her warning yell came at the same time as the knife cut into Adam's arm. He fell, landing on his back. After which, the three cowards ran toward their beat up two-door vehicle. She heard them peel away as she practically sprinted to where Adam lay on the ground, and knelt down by his side as soon as she reached him.

"Oh God, Adam. Please, please be okay," she sobbed. "Help!" There was so much blood. She ran her hands over his torso to see where else they might have stabbed him. Had she missed it?

"It's not mine," he said hoarsely.

This time she sobbed in relief and hugged him. The knife sticking out of his arm, however, was proof that at least some of the blood was his.

Just then the security guard ran over to them. "Where were you?" she yelled at him accusingly.

"The ambulance is on its way," he said. He looked terrified.

Emeline was pissed. "We need a better security team down here," she snapped.

"Done," Adam said.

She wasn't sure if she should pull the knife out, but decided she wouldn't chance hurting him more by pulling it out herself. He, on the other hand, decided he no longer wanted it stuck in his body, and pulled it out. She took her sweater off, bunched it up, and pressed it against his arm.

"Did they hurt you?" Adam asked, looking up at her tenderly.

She shook her head. "I'm not the one who got a knife stuck in my arm.

He winced, and she sobbed louder, a tear falling on his cheek. He closed his eyes and shook his head. "If I had been even a minute later."

"Not your fault, Adam. Please don't blame yourself."

"I had extra security put in the lobby, more cameras installed…" He trailed off.

She looked up angrily at the security guard. Had he been paying attention to the monitors, he may have spotted the three men approaching her. He wore a gun at his side for God's sake. Adam must have hired cops who often took secondary security jobs.

The ambulance finally arrived, and Emeline got in with him, holding his hand all the way to the hospital. Fortunately, the wound wasn't deep. A few stiches, some painkillers, and antibiotics, the doctor said, and Adam would be fine. And Adam had not been lying about the rest of the blood not being his. He had gotten *them* all good.

"Where did you learn to fight like that?" she asked him as the doctor was stitching him up.

"Been at it for a while," he said through gritted teeth.

"I'm sorry. Don't try and talk right now," she said wincing in sympathy and tightening the hold she had on his hand. She hadn't left his side since they arrived, except to briefly call her father to let him know she wasn't coming today. She didn't go into specifics, not wanting him to worry. The security guard had managed to do one thing by retrieving her purse for her.

"It's okay." Another wince. "I need the

distraction." He took a deep breath and remained quiet for a few seconds before speaking again. "I lived a bit of a nomadic lifestyle for several years, and mixed martial arts was my constant." He gave her a sad smile. "I got to the point in life where I needed an escape. Even from myself. Anyway, the discipline and training were good for my soul, and I much preferred it to solely working out at the gym."

Emeline was impressed. He had the grace of a panther with the way he had moved his body. And she was touched that he shared that piece of himself with her. She had wondered why he fell off the face of the Earth for a while, but she just had no idea that escaping himself was the reason behind it. God, there was so much she didn't know about him, so much she had said that she wished she could take back. "Adam, I—"

A police officer walked in to take a statement from them. Adam's jaw was locked, tense, as she recounted the events of what happened. He then recounted his own version from when he got there, and they both gave descriptions of the three men, although the footage from the garage would serve even better for identifying the culprits.

When both the police officer and the doctor left the room, Adam said, "Why is it that you and I seem to find ourselves in hospitals together after work? If you wanted to see me out of the office, a coffee shop, or a bar for drinks would be much more preferable." He gave her a small smile, and she gave him one in return right before more tears slid down her cheeks. "Hey, none of that now."

"Oh, Adam. I'm so sorry. It's all my fault."

He looked incredulous. "Your fault that three men attacked you? If anything, the fault is mine. I will have more than one security guard down in the garage, even after hours. Better yet, you are never walking down there alone."

She was touched by his concern, especially given what she had said to him earlier. "I didn't mean what I said to you. Please believe me. I was upset, but not at you, and then I got annoyed at your comment and was intentionally cruel to you. I am so sorry." In a rush she added, "And I certainly don't take people for spins, I mean not that you're not … and it's been two years since I've even … oh God." Adam's eyebrow shot up at her admission, and she felt her face flame. Then he smiled, a heart-stoppingly beautiful smile she had longed to see from him since that first day at the office, and she hoped that it meant he had forgiven her. "I don't see you that way, you know."

"What way is that?" he asked, though she suspected he knew what she meant.

Still, she owed it to him to let him know what she *did* see. "I think you're honest and genuine, and even though you come off a bit gruff, you truly have a kind heart. As far as paying people to like you, I believe you'd sooner pay them to fuck off."

He chuckled at that and squeezed the hand that he was still holding. "Thank you for saying that and for staying with me," he said sincerely.

"I'm the one who should be thanking *you*, Adam." She leaned over and kissed his cheek. Their gazes locked when she pulled back. She could feel his warm breath on her face. "I was so scared." Her voice trembled. "Thank you for saving me."

"I almost didn't get to you in time." He closed the small space between them and put his forehead against hers.

She was scared for another reason now, and her heart beat frantically, her emotions going haywire. He could have been stabbed fatally, all because of coming to her rescue, and the last words she would have ever said to him would have been cruel ones. The idea of never seeing him again felt like a stab to her heart. She hadn't even realized how deep her feelings ran until now, and if he didn't feel the same, it might crush her. They were too close now, breathing each other's breath. The desire to kiss his lips was overwhelming her.

"I can't ride a bicycle," she blurted.

"Excuse me?" he pulled back to look at her. When she didn't dispel what she had said, his jaw dropped. "You're joking."

She shrugged.

"Why have you never learned?"

That part actually made her sad to think of and as if understanding, he gave her hand another squeeze. "Tell me."

"I'm really terrible at it, to be honest."

"Come on. It can't be that bad."

"Trust me, if there's a tree, or some sort of ditch or something, I instantly become a magnet towards it."

He chuckled. "I guess the term 'as easy as riding a bike,' doesn't apply to you then?"

They both laughed at that. When she got quiet, he asked, "What is it?"

She'd never told anyone this story, but somehow in this moment it felt right to open up to him a little, especially given what they had just been through and the fact that she had taken out her shortcomings on him when all he wanted was to do something nice for the staff.

"I don't think I had a normal childhood growing up." Emeline shook her head, recalling the memories, sadly, fondly. She bent her head, keeping her gaze locked on their joined hands. A sense of rightness filled her.

"My parents didn't usually take me to the park to go on swings and jungle gyms, or out for ice cream, not really even to the movies. We went boating, ate crepes, and saw Broadway plays. We went to Tuscany instead of Disneyworld. We read books on weekends, played Trivial Pursuit. It was amazing," she ended wistfully.

"One day when I was about six years old, my dad glanced up from grading papers and said, 'We should teach her how to ride a bicycle.' Over the next week, we discovered how awful I was." Memories of scraped knees and the too up-close smell of dirt, or freshly mowed grass filled her senses. She did well with the training wheels, but once they came off, it was as she had said about being a magnet for injury by any ridiculous means. "After so many failed attempts, I said I didn't want to do it anymore. And then one day when I was eight, I told my father I wanted to try again. He had planned to give me a lesson the next day, but my mom went into labor."

She glanced up at Adam to find him staring at her intently, his eyes full of sadness.

"We hadn't thought she would go into labor yet. It was too soon." Emeline never asked for lessons after that.

"What happened to them?"

"My mother died in childbirth, and my brother was stillborn."

"We should be four," he muttered. "Jesus, I am so sorry. That day at the cemetery..."

Emeline nodded. "I couldn't sleep the night before. I hear my little brother crying sometimes when I'm dreaming, even though he never had the chance to cry. And that day marked the twentieth anniversary of their deaths." She told him how she had gone to the cemetery practically in the middle of the night and accidentally fallen asleep. She had even told him in more detail about her recurring nightmare, the same one he had woken her up from.

His good arm encircled her, and he brought her close to him. They sat their holding each other until Adam was released. Somehow, she knew that Adam understood her pain all too well.

Chapter Nine

"No, no, no! You should never ride a bicycle again," Adam said angrily as he hoisted Emeline up from the pavement. "Seriously, every bike shop in town should have a picture of you in their window with a warning caption saying, 'Do not let this woman rent or buy a bike.' Let me see." He took her hand in his and turned it over to examine it. Her palm was all scratched up and bleeding in several places.

Emeline was glad that her head, elbows, and knees were well protected, because everything else on her, if not scraped, would be sore for at least a week, especially her poor behind. She had managed many ungraceful landings in the past few hours.

****

News had spread like wildfire around the office regarding the attack and Adam's heroics on Monday. Even Melody had found out and wanted to use it as publicity, *Hero Boss at Publishing Enchanted Saves Employee*, but Adam forbade it. It was kept quiet and out of the press, and by mid-week, they had a suspect in custody, one who squealed like a pig. The other two were caught shortly after. Just when Emeline felt safe again, a major bomb was dropped on her.

The three men had been *paid* to rough her up.

Soren Grover—he had been the one to knock her purse out of her hand—had pointed the finger, not only at his two accomplices in exchange for a reduced sentence, and given the fact that he never actually laid a hand on her, he would get it, but had also accused Jarod of orchestrating the attack in order to play the hero. Furthermore, Soren had let it be known that one of the accomplices bragged about receiving a nice chunk of change for roughing up some old dude in Long Island.

Emeline had felt sick to her stomach and was glad that she had Adam down at the police station with her. He had been fuming mad. It was one thing to suspect Jarod might have hurt her father, but to hear it confirmed made her see red. Still, it was the word of a junkie, since there was no actual physical evidence to tie Jarod to her father's assault, and there was also no proof that the bastard was hiding in the garage as Soren had claimed. He wasn't clearly identifiable in any of the footage from the surveillance, but it was enough to go on for Emeline to get a restraining order against him and for Adam to get his ass fired while the investigation continued.

Jarod had called her the next day, his voice bitter and angry. "You fucking bitch. You and your boyfriend ruined my life. I got fired."

"That's nothing compared to what you deserve, you sick son of a bitch," she had yelled. Christina had been unsure of whether or not to put him through to her, but Emeline insisted. She needed to give him a piece of her mind. "You should be rotting in jail for what you did to my father, for what you did to me, for what you let those..."

"Your father should not have spoken to me with such disrespect! Yet, there was barely a scratch on him."

"You ass—"

"And you weren't in any real danger, Emeline," he scoffed. "I was about to stop them when that animal showed up."

She gritted her teeth. "They put their hands on me. I was so fucking scared thinking they were about to rape me, all so you could play your little game of rescuing the damsel in distress. You piece of shit! *You're* the animal!"

"You can't prove anything." His voice turned calculatingly cold. "Grover was a junkie I couldn't get off back in my rookie days. He has a vendetta against me, along with my jealous ex-girlfriend."

"You're insane. I was never your girlfriend. They will find proof. And by all means, keep calling my office where I can have witnesses to your harassment and violation of your restraining order. I'll be informing the police of this call." She hung up before he could spew another vile word.

Adam had come in a few minutes later to find her shaking. He had crouched down by her chair and held her hands as she told him what transpired.

"Don't take any more calls from him, okay?"

Emeline nodded.

"I've told Christina to keep a detailed log of his calls." He had hugged her tightly until her heartbeat returned to normal, and when it finally did, he had asked, "Do you have plans on Sunday?"

"I should be back from my dad's around three."

"Three it is," was all he had said.

****

Adam had told her to meet him on the Upper East Side. He looked absolutely amazing with his hair pulled back, his tight-fitting t-shirt that accentuated all of his bulging muscles, and his army green cargo shorts, which revealed his long, lean, muscular legs. He had made her mouth water. It surprised her that the chilly weather had no effect on him, but then again, he had all of those muscles to keep him warm, she thought. She, on the other hand, wore a pair of long black leggings, a fitted scoop neck t-shirt, and a zip up sweater, and although she was way more covered up than he was, she did not miss the way his gaze roamed up and down her body in appreciation.

Two bike rentals, and hours' worth of lessons later, she actually found his frustration with her amusing, especially given his initial persistence stating that he could definitely teach her how to ride.

"I never thought I would say this, Emeline, but you are unteachable."

She laughed at that and then cringed when she straightened fully.

"Where does it hurt?" he asked as he held her at arm's length and looked her over.

"Where *doesn't* it hurt?"

Adam breathed out heavily. "We're done here." He took her un-scraped hand in his, practically ordered her to sit on a bench while he returned the bikes, and then led her out of the park. "I live nearby," he told her, making her forget all about her injuries, spiking up her heart rate.

His apartment was spacious, three bedrooms, he told her when she asked, although she hadn't asked to see any of them. She was afraid of what she might do if she actually saw his bedroom. He explained that he used the other two as an office and an exercise room. The large foyer led into a living room, with a kitchen and dining area to the left, and the hallway to the bedrooms on the right. The floors were dark wood, beautifully polished, and the décor seemed to have popped right out of a Pottery Barn catalogue and nestled itself into his apartment. A large white leather sectional sat in the living room, complete with accent chairs, pillows, and a throw blanket, and beautifully complemented by a glass coffee table, brown shag area rug, and an electric fireplace with a TV mounted on the wall above it. There were a few knickknacks scattered throughout, but no photographs.

He placed his hand on the small of her back—his touch sending electrifying pulses up and down her spine—and led her to sit down on the couch while he went rummaging for a first aid kit. "I had an interior designer do all this," he said as he kneeled down in front of her on the couch.

Made sense, she thought, unless he had a secret talent for interior design. "It's beautiful. Wish I had thought of hiring one." Not that she didn't love her one-bedroom apartment. It was cozy, and she kept it fairly neat and organized, but the layout had more to do with functionality and space-saving than Feng Shui, being that she could fit several of her apartments in his. Still, her place was quite a nice size for the price and location. He seemed pleased with her compliment.

"Thank you." He took a cotton swab and dipped it into hydrogen peroxide before gently applying it to her scrapes. It stung, making her flinch. He brought her palm close to his lips and blew on it, and she actually inhaled sharply, but not because it hurt. Her insides curled with heat, and she shivered.

Adam glanced up at her with a knowing smile. "Are you cold?"

"No," she replied in a breathy whisper.

Next came the antibiotic ointment, followed by more blowing. Emeline had to close her eyes this time until the excited quiver passed through her body. Heat rose to her cheeks. Fortunately, he didn't look up at her this time. Instead, he continued with his tender attention, applying gauze to her palm and taping it up neatly. When he removed her shoe and sock to examine her ankle, she had to bite down on her lip to keep from moaning at the feel of his hands caressing her.

"I think it's just a slight sprain," he said, finally looking up at her. He still held onto her foot as he spoke, one hand on her calf.

"Why don't you have any photographs?" she asked him softly. She was genuinely curious, wanting to know more about him, but she wanted to keep from making a fool of herself by jumping him at this moment as well. It was as if her libido had been asleep for some time and reawakened with ferocity like a dragon catching a thief in its lair.

His eyes turned sad, making her instantly regret asking. The last thing she wanted to do was cause him pain. "It's okay. You don't have to tell me."

He shrugged, let go of her foot, and then sat beside her on the couch. "They're just painful reminders of the past."

"No selfies for you on Instagram then?" She chuckled, wanting to lighten the mood, but then a memory assaulted her.

"What is it?"

Emeline shook her head. "Nothing. You just reminded me of someone."

"Who?" He took her hand in his. Something on her face must have given him cause for concern.

She locked gazes with him, sadness twisting in her gut. "Just a boy in a story my mother used to tell me when I was little." The boy did have a photograph, a painting rather, of his parents. In the story, he had spoken to them at night until he had grown, and then he, too, had rid himself of it and all of the paintings in the castle.

"It wasn't a very happy story then, was it?"

He hit the nail on the head and the comparison he made did not go unnoticed, making her feel for the little boy Adam had been.

"No. But it had a happy ending."

"Maybe you can tell it to me one day." He slid off the couch to kneel in front of her again and put her sock and shoe back on. "For now, I don't know about you, but I'm starving, and a little bit traumatized by what I have witnessed today."

This time she gave him a full-blown laugh right before he disappeared into the kitchen. For a moment, she thought he was about to start cooking, and envisioned how hot he would look, shirtless, standing by the stove, completely focused on the task one minute, while stealing heated glances in her direction another.

She was sharply snapped out of her fantasy when he held up several menus for her to choose from. He admitted to not being a good cook, and sadly, neither was she.

They had settled on Chinese food, ordering enough to probably keep them fed for several days, though both of them simultaneously agreed the food would need to be discarded the next day. It wasn't a date, but Emeline couldn't remember the last time she had this much fun having dinner with someone she *was* on a date with. She found herself laughing practically throughout the entire meal as he went over, in great detail, the late afternoon's debacle.

When they finished eating, he drove her home and then held her hand as he walked her to the elevator. Her heart pounded as the doors opened, wondering if he would kiss her and what that would mean for them if he did.

No, it wasn't a date, but God, she wanted it to be.

"Thank you for today, Adam." She gave him a half smile before she stepped into the elevator, his heated gaze burning in her memory.

Chapter Ten

Emeline was going to be the death of him. He ached so badly for her, so much so, he thought he might burst from the need to touch her, kiss her. He had seen how her body reacted to him, and knew that she was just as affected. He wanted more than just a night with her though, or several meaningless ones for that matter, but he was at a loss. She worked for him. He'd had a fling with someone at his previous endeavor, which didn't go so well for the woman and left him feeling awful for it.

What would her coworkers think of her if they started dating? And what would happen if things did not go well for them? He worried that she'd quit and then he'd never see her again. The idea of that actually happening felt like a sharper stab than the one he had gotten from the knife.

Then there was Folgen to deal with. Emeline had way too much on her plate right now, and Adam worried about the toll it was taking on her. The bastard would be smart for now and keep his distance, he thought, but it was far from over. One way or another, he was going to be held accountable for what he had done to Emeline and her father. Adam would see to it.

Holding her, touching her, had been as easy as breathing for him, and seeing her get viciously attacked sent him into the kind of rage he had never known he was capable of having. For the first time in his life, he felt a connection with someone that ran so deep, he could feel it in his bones.

She saw him. All of him. And she saw through him, making him feel raw in front of her. And whether by choice, or because she felt the same pull to him as he did to her, his flesh and blood apparition had been slowly revealing all of herself to him.

He saw her, too.

Their relationship had been tumultuous since their first meeting. Every time they had moved towards a truce, something would occur to stir one of them up, but ever since the attack, they had grown closer, and both of their armors had been slowly falling away piece by metallic piece. He had wanted her smiles, and now he got them. Sweet and shy before the bicycle fiasco on Sunday, and now, this week, they could barely look at each other without breaking into laughter. He also did not miss the way she'd glanced at him when she thought he wasn't looking, with her eyes hooded. He nearly moaned out loud in a meeting when out of the corner of his eye, he saw her biting her lips several times. He wanted to yell at everyone to clear the fuck out of the room so he could ravish her atop the table. Suffice it to say, he needed to remain seated until everyone, including Emeline, had cleared out so that he would not embarrassingly reveal the bulge in his pants.

He had been guilty of ogling her his fair share as well, what with the sexy skirts she often wore. They may have been a professionally modest length, but they hugged her curves beautifully and showed enough leg to remind him how it felt when he had caressed one of hers on Sunday. Then there was her scent that drove him completely insane when she was near, with her soft, floral perfume and herbal shampoo. She made him feel primal, like an animal in heat, hard and wanting. He wanted to run his fingers through her soft hair as he buried his face into her neck.

"Adam?" Emeline opened the door to his office. "Sorry, I knocked, but you didn't answer."

Shit. He cleared his throat. The bulge against his black tailored pants was actually causing him a great deal of discomfort.

"Are you all right?" she asked. "You look flushed." She walked over to him around his desk, which fortunately hid his bottom half, and she touched his forehead with the back of her hand. "Hmm. No fever."

On the one hand, he was beyond thrilled that she felt comfortable enough to interact with him so easily now, but on the other, her touch right now may drive him further into madness. He may just swipe everything off his desk and have his way with her like he had pictured doing a million times since he met her.

She saved him from doing something rash by going around to sit in the chair facing him. That's when he noticed the several papers she was holding.

"It's just warm in here," he said by way of explanation. "I run a littler hotter than some." *Fuck!* Again, he nearly groaned as she bit her lip. He jutted his chin out toward her papers. "What's that?"

"Oh." She looked at the papers as if noticing for the first time that she had them. "I just wanted to give you an update for the coffee shop. Just tossed some ideas around with my team." Adam saw a mischievous smile spread across her face. "This time I delivered them myself."

He leaned forward and snatched the printed sheets from her. "Smart ass." He read through the promotions and liked what they came up with, and after he made a minor tweak, one that she approved of as well, he was pleased. "I am glad you stopped by." *For more than just a work-related reason.* "What do you think of the website so far?"

"I love it. It's generating quite a few hits, and I think that once we do a sneak peek of the coffee shop with discounts and such, it will generate even more. Also, readers and our authors keep responding favorably to the new genres. Our acquisition editors are super excited over several new submissions they found to be extremely promising."

He loved how her entire face lit up when she talked about something she was passionate about, and he envied that. He liked what he did, and he was damn good at it, but he never found himself fulfilled by it, at least not until he bought Publishing Enchanted, though he surmised it had quite a bit to do with the beauty sitting before him. He found himself caring about the people who worked here, too, and about creating excitement and being proud of something he helped to produce. This job was actually rewarding beyond monetarily, although, *that* particular reward would be approaching soon enough. And for the first time, even thinking about selling this company in the future felt as if he'd be selling something precious to him, something he didn't want someone else to get their hands on.

"Huh. Go figure."

"What?"

He didn't realize he had said it aloud. He brushed it off as nothing and finished the discussion, finally focusing on more than just her supple lips moving. When they were done with their discussion, Emeline surprised him with an invitation.

"So, there is this great bar a few blocks down that has karaoke night on Thursday. A bunch of us are going." She paused as if gauging his reaction. "Do you maybe want to come?"

To say that he was both surprised and touched was an understatement. No one from work had ever invited him out before. He had always been the unapproachable boss who went to business dinners with other stuffed suits. And usually his attendance at bars was solo. He couldn't help the smile that spread across his face at her hopeful expression. She actually wanted him there. "Thank you. I'd love to come."

Not that he had ever gotten up and sung at a karaoke bar before. Actually, he hadn't sung since his junior high school band days in the States, unless it was to the music in his car, but he'd get up and make a fool of himself for Emeline if it made her smile.

They walked over to the bar together after work. Emeline's team members and a few other staff were already there since he and Emeline had stayed at the office later. He felt a stab of jealousy when he saw her face light up at the sight of a tall, though a bit on the skinny side, man with dark hair and blue eyes. Adam couldn't see what the fuss was about, but the guy was garnering quite a bit attention from several of her coworkers. And then Emeline sprinted over to him and nearly tackled him in a hug.

He had the sudden urge to rip the guy's arms off when he took Emeline's face in his hands and gave her a kiss on each cheek. He heard them speaking in French when he got closer.

"You big sneak," she said to him. "That's why you asked me where I was going when I spoke to you earlier."

The guy threw his head back and laughed and then he hugged her tightly again. "I missed your silly face."

Adam locked gazes with DeAnne, who pressed her lips together, trying to suppress a smile. He wondered what she had seen on his face. Christina, the normally shy assistant, smacked her in the shoulder. He had missed part of the conversation with the distraction, but he caught the part about the guy sleeping over at Emeline's house tonight. Adam felt like such a fool. How could he have misunderstood her feelings so completely? He wondered if she were that callous to invite another man to sleep over her house in front of him, knowing full well that he understood French. Or perhaps, she wasn't being cruel at all. She just may have never thought of him as anything more than a friend.

His blood was boiling with his own jealousy, an emotion so completely foreign to him when it came to the opposite sex, as he'd never cared before. He wanted to leave before he did something stupid, something he had no right to do since Emeline wasn't his.

He was about to make up an excuse to leave when Emeline turned in his direction and gave him a beaming smile. "Adam," she said, "Come meet my cousin."

He could feel the huge grin on DeAnne's face without even having to look at her. She had known all along he was her cousin and just caught him acting like a childish idiot. Still, he felt as if the huge, crushing weight on his chest had been lifted. Mercifully, both Emeline and her cousin seemed oblivious to his inner tantrum.

He walked over to where they stood and shook hands with Phillippe Bell, who had apparently not been expected until Sunday. "Adam Charmont. Nice to meet you."

"Charmont? It is French, no?"

When Adam confirmed his French ancestry and the fact that he both understood and spoke the language, Phillippe clapped him on the back good-naturedly and when he got to chatting with the bloke over a drink with Emeline sitting in between them, he found that he actually liked him. He no longer minded that some of the female acquaintances were swooning over his heavily accented English as long as the girl in the middle was swooning over him.

Adam couldn't help but laugh as Emeline and her cousin sang a duet on stage. Her voice was actually pretty decent, hitting mostly the right notes, but Phillippe was awful, and he kept laughing. Still they both looked like they were having a great time doing it, and Adam was very much enjoying the view of a slightly tipsy brunette swaying to the music.

DeAnne moved over to sit beside him. "Enjoying the show, boss man?"

Adam arched a brow in her direction.

"Me, personally, I wanted popcorn earlier." She laughed and patted his shoulder. "I wouldn't wait too long if I were you. The next one may not be her cousin."

He didn't have a chance to respond since the song Emeline was singing ended and DeAnne, Rhonda, and Christine got up to sing, "It's Raining Men". Not that he knew how to respond to DeAnne's comment anyway. As much as he wanted to drag Emeline away and claim her as his, they had the real world to deal with. At least that's what he kept telling himself as an excuse, because if he was being honest with himself, he was scared shitless. His feelings for her ran deep, and that gave her the power to destroy him.

Emeline and Phillippe rejoined their table, giggling as they sat down. The girls on stage didn't sound half bad, and actually the quietest one of them all, Christina, had the loudest voice. That girl carried a tune quite well.

"I need to pee," Emeline stated with a giggle.

"Such a lightweight," Phillippe said to her in French. Turning to Adam he switched to English. "I can drink her under the table, I believe the expression is." He then downed the rest of his beer. "So, Adam, she has not said, but I think she met someone. It is you?"

For a brief moment, he thought perhaps she did meet someone, but then again, he had already been mistaken about her cousin. Since he had no answer he could give, he settled for asking a question instead. "If she hasn't said anything, how do you know she met someone?"

"We don't see each other often, my cousin and I," he began, "but we speak a lot. I've never heard such a happiness in her voice in a long time. Not since we were children and she lost her mama."

It was a bittersweet description of how she was feeling, but the revelation nearly knocked the breath out of him. "We aren't dating, if that's what you're asking." Adam heard his own disappointment in his response.

Phillippe seemed to study him for a moment before he spoke again. "You will take good care of her, yes?"

"Yes."

Phillippe nodded, seemingly satisfied. It was a promise Adam intended to keep. He was going to find a way to win her heart, and a way to let go of the past so he could give her his.

The ladies finished their song and rejoined them, and Emeline came back to the table shortly after, just in time to hear the tail end of Joe's rendition of "Can't Help Falling in Love," which he sang to his pregnant wife. His voice was quite terrible, completely off-key, but his wife wore a beaming smile the entire time he sang.

When it was Adam's turn, he chose Pink Floyd's "Comfortably Numb," one of his favorite songs of all time, and one befitting him, though he never needed either the *pinprick* or *fever* to feel the way he did. He searched for her in the crowd while he sang and noticed her staring back at him, her lips slightly parted. She seemed a bit awestruck, which encouraged him to keep going. It was his past, his confession, and he wondered if she got it.

He no longer wanted to be numb.

Loud clapping and cheers rang around the bar when he finished, along with catcalls from several women, possibly a man or two, but he ignored them all, heading straight for the seat next to Emeline.

"Wow, Adam. You have such a beautiful voice," Rhonda told him.

"Thank you."

Emeline placed a hand on his shoulder and leaned in to whisper in his ear. "That was really amazing. I didn't know you could sing."

When he turned his head towards her, they were so close that their noses almost touched. He felt the breath she had let out against his face. It was warm and smelled like the fruity gum she had been chewing since she came back from the bathroom. He noticed she had reapplied her lip gloss as well, making her plump lips shine in the muted light, lips he wanted so badly to devour even though they had an audience.

He leaned into her instead, using any reason to be close to her. "It's been a while, but I'm glad you liked it."

No one noticed their exchange since their party's attention was on the next singer, who was receiving cheers and jeers for his drunken solo. At the end of the night, he saw Emeline and Phillippe to a cab before getting in his own. He then thought about the call he was going to make in the morning to Sabine and then later to Melody. They'd both be pissed. Sabine more than likely would pull out of the event, but he had a different vision, a better one, with the way he wanted Saturday to go.

Chapter Eleven

"Comfortably Numb" blasted in surround sound for the third time in a row as Emeline drove from her father's house in Long Island to the triathlon event in New Jersey Saturday morning. Phillippe would be splitting his time between her place and her dad's for the week, but today they had some manly bonding time and Emeline wanted them to have it. It gave her father a sense of what it would have been like had his own son survived, but he and his nephew were also very close. Phillippe's father, her uncle, had always been too absorbed in his own life to be much of a father figure, and therefore her dad had stepped in whenever he could, and practically every summer since Emeline was a child was spent with him in either Paris or New York. She had always treasured her summers abroad.

The song was coming to an end, but Emeline had set it on repeat, letting it play again. She couldn't help picturing Adam's haunting voice as he sang on stage, the top few buttons of his shirt undone, and his falsetto notes sending chills up and down her body. It was as if he had been singing only to her and everyone else at the bar had just faded away.

A laugh escaped her when flashes of last Sunday's bike lesson fiasco suddenly popped into her head. The image of him crooning, shifted to him staring at her in complete disbelief at her lack of balance on two wheels, and then to him jumping off his bike and chasing her for several yards so that he could save her from crashing into a tree.

She had finally agreed to participate in today's events, especially since he banned her from the first leg of the race, which for this particular event would be biking. She'd be starting with boating and ending with the run to the finish line. The fact that she was skipping part of the race disqualified her from winning, and because of that, she decided to enter as a solo act. She didn't mind, however. This was all in good fun anyway with the added bonus of not having to embarrass herself.

Not wishing to make herself sick of the Pink Floyd song, Emeline hit shuffle on a playlist on her iPhone. She kept imagining Adam singing some of them to her, sometimes with more of his buttons undone, and she blasted the music in her car up until she found a parking spot.

The entire place was packed. Signs and banners advertising both the triathlon and the publishing company were everywhere, along with snack stands and porta-potties. She stopped at the Publishing Enchanted kiosk to make sure all the books and brochures were displayed the way she had wanted and found that the interns had done an amazing job. She then went over to the welcome station to sign in and pick up her sticker.

Adam was waiting there for her with a smile on his face. "I already registered you." He handed her the sticker, which she noticed had the same number printed as the one Adam had already stuck on his Publishing Enchanted t-shirt. Behind him was a tandem bike.

"But I thought—"

"Change of plans," he said. "I'm partnering with you today."

"What about Sabine?"

Adam shrugged. "She can't make it after all." He paused for a moment before adding. "Actually, she threw a bit of a hissy fit and said she would not be attending today." He shrugged again, his smile never wavering, and her butterflies did somersaults, knowing that he wanted to partner with her instead of Sabine.

And to top it all off, this was one of the nicest

things anyone had ever done for her. He saved her from either making a complete fool of herself or having to repeatedly come up with some lame excuse about why she wouldn't be biking. Emeline had no idea what to say except, "Thank you." She was too choked up, however, to return his smile, but she gathered that he understood just how much what he did for her meant.

"Just let me do all the work," he added with a snort before tugging her out of the way of the line forming behind her.

They had some time before the race would officially begin, so they both went and did their separate duties, greeting people. Emeline found her work team. None of them seemed surprised at her having teamed up with Adam, and DeAnne kept throwing an impish gaze in her direction and even came over to give her a hip bump.

She found Melody *bup, bupping* around, seemingly over what probably was a disappointment to her—the lack of a celebrity in attendance, especially given that Sabine was coming as a *personal favor* to her.

Finally, she heard the announcement over a megaphone that the competition was about to begin, and she headed over to Adam, who was already positioned at the starting line.

He tipped the bike toward her, balancing it, so she could climb on. Then he turned around to face her. "Just hold on to the handle bars, and I'll do the rest." He gave her a wink and then turned back around to face the front.

And what a nice view she had to look at. She admired his broad shoulders, well defined back muscles, and strong arms. He had held her in those arms on several occasions—in the hospital, at her desk, when he had picked her up off the ground repeatedly—making her feel safe, cherished even. Then there was his mouthwatering masculine scent, a mixture of some subtle woodsy spice and freshly laundered clothes, with a hint of coconut coming from his hair, currently styled in a messy bun atop his head. She had never really cared for the man bun, until now that she was seeing it on him. He usually just wore it down, and only seldom pulled back in a ponytail. She had the constant urge to run her fingers through it, to find out if it really was as soft as it looked.

Emeline wanted to forgo the damn race and find a quiet little spot where they could ravish each other instead. She then thought about the fact that the stupid bike had handlebars for her when she wanted nothing more than to wrap her arms around him and hold him tight.

"On your mark…"

"You ready?" Adam asked her at the same time the announcer said "Get set…"

"Yep," she replied. Her part was easy. She had a fine back to admire.

"Go!"

Adam easily weaved his way in and around the other bikers. Even with her added weight, they were steadily in either the lead or within second or third place. No wonder he had thought that he could teach her. Adam was great at it, lithely maneuvering the larger beast and bending it to his will, and she actually found herself having fun on two wheels for the first time in her life.

They didn't finish first, but the order didn't count yet. She and Adam sprinted for the boats, and this time she was able to assist him. They moved quickly, racing toward the front of the line when suddenly, he slowed his pace exponentially.

"Tired already, big guy?" she asked.

"Nah. Since we're not really eligible to win, might as well enjoy the company." He threw her another sexy wink over his shoulder.

He also had a point. She was enjoying his company very much, not to mention getting a good view of the front of him when he flipped around in the seat to face her. She continued to row backward until he turned them around so that his back was facing the forward direction and he told her to relax.

She giggled. "How very gentlemanly of you. All I need now is a large sun hat and an umbrella."

He threw his head back and laughed. "I'll get you one next time."

Next time. She wouldn't read into what he meant by those words or if he even realized what he was saying, but she liked the unconscious thought popping into his head if that was the case, nonetheless, especially since she had often been thinking of *next time* as well.

Warmth spread to her cheeks as she watched his biceps contract. The smile on his face was carefree, far different than the serious expression he often wore at work, and then his expression morphed into what she could only describe as one of desire. Their gazes locked, his eyes hooded. She felt her heart rate spike, and despite the chill in the air, her skin felt flushed.

"They have ice-skating here in the winter," he said, his voice coming out a little gravelly. "It's not as crowded as in the city."

She didn't mean to laugh at him. Not at all. And at the moment, she wasn't examining his invitation as being a date or just a friendly outing as karaoke had been. Instead, she was trying to collect her bearings, to stop laughing long enough to tell him…

"Holy Jesus, you can't bloody ice-skate either." He deduced it on his own. He shook his head. "I shudder to think of you on skis and snowboards for that matter."

"I shudder to think of all the broken bones I'd

have. Trust me. I don't get it, either. I seem to be well balanced on my own two feet, and I am even pretty graceful on heels, if I do say so myself."

"I've noticed," he said as his heated gaze returned.

They came in almost last this time, and then they started the final leg of the race, running, way behind quite a few teams.

He jogged beside her, barely breaking a sweat, even though he had been doing all the heavy lifting thus far. She, on the other hand, had it easy up until now and was already starting to feel a stitch forming in her side. "I really need to get in better shape."

She could have sworn she heard him mumble something about her being shaped just fine, and again, that caused a heat to unfurl within her that had nothing to do with her exertion.

She definitely did not imagine his smart-ass comment of, "I'm happy this portion requires only your own two feet."

She mocked punched him in the shoulder and he feigned being hurt, so she did it harder the next time, and to her shock, he threw her over his shoulder and ran a few yards with her that way, laughing at her as she begged for him to put her down, despite part of her craving for him to keep touching her.

How different things had gotten between them. They had always been so serious around each other, and now Emeline couldn't help laughing or smiling whenever she was in his company, and sometimes even when she wasn't. She felt lighter.

She had no idea what place they came in, only that their team was one of the last, nor did she care. As it turned out, Rhonda and her family, consisting of her husband and three children, came in first, and a sulking

Joe and his team, additionally comprised of DeAnne and Christina, came in second.

"Oh my God. I'm going to have to hear about this for a month," she said to Adam. She imagined Joe picking apart the entire race to try to figure out what error was made in order for him to lose. That man was beyond competitive and a bit of a sore loser it seemed. Teasing him about it would just be added fun.

When the race was over, mostly everyone, especially staff who brought their families, stayed to have a picnic in the park. Publishing Enchanted had supplied the food. Emeline and Adam sat with her team, and even Melody came over to join them. Emeline hated to admit it, but when Melody wasn't making her blood boil by flirting with Adam, she was actually kind of entertaining and not as fake as Emeline had thought at first. There had to be some sort of façade one had to project in this business, she supposed, and despite some of the mundaneness about her, Melody was extremely shrewd and business savvy.

Everyone finally started to disperse when it began getting dark out. Adam walked Emeline to her car. She decided to go home, take a long shower, and sleep tonight instead of going back to her father's house. She'd see him and her cousin tomorrow instead.

"Drive safe. See you Monday," Adam told her as he held the driver's side door of her car open for her.

She smiled and waved as she drove away.

Ending a fabulous day stuck in heavy traffic definitely put a bit of a damper on her mood, but seeing Jarod outside of her apartment building when she got home made it even worse.

"You are violating the restraining order," she spat at him. She took comfort in the fact that if she screamed, someone would definitely hear her and that though it was already fully dark out, it wasn't all that late.

She made as if to ignore and bypass him into her building, but he grabbed her wrist and pushed her against the side of the brick, away from the view of the doorman in the lobby. "I want you to retract everything, Emeline." She was about to scream, but he put his hand over her mouth. "You will call my office and explain that your new boyfriend is crazy and he made everything up. You will apologize to my boss profusely. Then you will tell the police that you acted in a jealous rage, conspiring with Soren against me. Do you understand?" He removed his hand from her mouth and placed it against her throat. "Because if you don't, I *will* make you regret it." His eyes were cold when he looked at her, and then the vile bastard actually kissed her. She tried to move her head, but he held her face painfully between his hands and then he let go and walked away.

She tasted bile. With her legs shaky and unsteady, she sank down to the ground and had no idea how long she stayed that way. It wasn't until her doorman, Ralph, came outside to smoke a cigarette that she finally moved.

He walked over to her and helped her to feet. "Are you hurt, Emeline?"

She shook her head. Physically, though still a little nauseated, she was fine.

Ralph looked concerned, though. "Can I call someone for you?"

Again, she shook her head, not sure she was capable of speech just yet. Ralph helped her inside, and finally she was able to tell him she just wanted to go upstairs.

She walked into her apartment, turned on the lights, and sank down to the floor, tears streaming down her face. She wanted to calm down a bit more before calling the police, to be rational enough to let them know every detail. Emeline decided she would not be bullied by him.

Her first call was not to the police, however. The thought of being alone right now, of talking to the police without him there with her, would be more than she could handle.

"Missed me already?" Adam asked when he answered, sounding as carefree as he had all day.

"Can you come over?" She heard the unsteadiness in her own voice and though she promised herself she would not cry in front of him, having already subjected him to her breakdowns before, her tears did not cooperate.

"What's wrong?" Now he sounded panicked.

Emeline couldn't speak, her tears suddenly choking her.

"Emeline, are you hurt?"

"No," she finally managed to say. "Jarod was here."

"I'll be right there," he said before the call ended.

As soon as she opened the door, he pulled her to him, and again, like a blubbering idiot, she let loose the tears, while finding safety and comfort in his embrace. After a few moments of just holding her and letting her cry, he pulled her over to the couch and she told him everything Jarod said. She had left out the part about him touching her.

"He fucking threatened you! I'm going to kill the bastard." Adam took out his cell phone and called his detective friend. When he ended the call, and looked at her, she saw a hatred so fierce in his eyes that for a moment she thought it was directed at her. He gently cupped her face and tilted it up just a little, exposing her throat. "I'm going to kill him," he repeated, his voice deadly. "He'd better pray the police find him first and lock him up."

Jarod had apparently left handprints on her throat.

"Please don't, Adam. Please. I couldn't bear anything happening to you."

"Shh, it's going to be okay." He hugged her close again. "Where else did he touch you?" When she didn't answer, he pulled away to look at her. "Where, Emeline?"

She couldn't lie to him. He saw it on her face and she would have to tell the detective anyway when he got there, so she told him everything. Adam's face turned red. He seemed about to yell, but Emeline was glad he didn't. He held her instead and didn't let go until the detective showed up to take her statement and he assured her that an APB had already been put out on Jarod. If he managed to find some way to avoid jail time for his first violation, a second would definitely ensure it. She silently sent up a thank you for whatever Herculean strength it took Adam to stay with her instead of chasing Jarod down himself and making good on his threat.

After the detective left, Adam refused to leave her, despite her telling him that she would be okay now.

"I'm either staying here, or dragging you back to my place," he insisted. "Your choice, but you're not staying alone tonight."

She lost track of how many times he had been there for her in the last few weeks. "Why is it that you're always there for me when I'm at my worst?" She thought about the first time she saw him, waking her up from a nightmare. She'd been stuck in one for the last twenty years, and here Adam was, constantly trying to pull her out of it. She only hoped that one day he would let her do the same for him.

"I'm glad I could be," he softly replied. "I want to see you through it. I feel..."

"What?" she asked when his pause stretched on.

"Drawn to you."

That was how she felt, too. Like something invisible pulling her toward him. Even now, sitting close to him on the couch, felt like a distance she wanted to cross. It was more than just a pull, however, she realized. So much more. She thought about his smile, his strength, his warmth, even his occasional gruffness, and the feeling of completeness washed over her, but she didn't say any of this to him.

"Me, too," was what she whispered while looking down at her hands resting on her thighs.

She made up the couch for him to sleep on. It wasn't what she longed for. Not at all. She wanted to fall asleep in his arms, to feel him surrounding her all night, and so much more, but this wasn't the way she wanted it to happen.

She would not allow fear and desperation to be a catalyst, not when it came to Adam.

Emeline was too far gone in love with him for that.

Chapter Twelve

She wouldn't say she had kept her distance from Adam, not physically anyway. They'd had lunches together, sometimes just the two of them, sometimes in a group, and they had a few dinners together, too, and to her delight, another karaoke night. Their work relationship had also been pretty smooth, with the occasional disagreement, but overall, she discovered they worked quite well together and the publishing house was thriving. The first café would be opening after the holidays, and already that first month was booked for signings. Jarod had fortunately not approached her again after his short stint in jail, but that could have also been due to the fact that Adam had been either escorting her home at night, or had a car take her home on late nights. Jarod was out on bail now. Not enough evidence to hold him with his compelling argument of "he said-she said-and the junkie said". He was free for the time being while the investigation was ongoing and the restraining order held firmly in place.

On the weekends that she went to see her father, he made sure to walk her to her car in the garage himself. Security had also been amped up with the hiring of extra guards per shift. Apparently, Adam's father had had bodyguards, smart given his wealth and the unwanted attention it could bring. Adam had refused to live that way, but then again, he kept a much lower profile than Senior had. He had been rethinking his decision now, but Emeline knew it was more for her sake and she felt guilty over it.

Emotionally, other than friendliness, she had tried for detachment, or at least the appearance of it, considering her discovery of her feelings for him. He was still so closed off from her that she couldn't get a read on him, but he was there for her. He was her friend. Sometimes, though, she'd catch glimmers of what she thought could be longing, and it made her wonder if perhaps he held back for some of the same reasons she did. The problem with being in love and having it unrequited felt like a fresh wound had opened in her heart, right next to the ones belonging to her mother and brother.

Adam hadn't asked her to accompany him to the ball, but neither of them used their plus one, which gave her a small sense of relief. Sabine would be there, Emeline knew that. However, he had never indicated they were going as a couple.

She took a cab, arriving before the girls and Joe. Rhonda would be bringing her husband, of course, and both DeAnne and Christina were bringing dates. Emeline was happy for them, and at least she'd have Joe at the table as sort of stand-in date since his wife, Jenna, was now mostly on bed rest. She had practically forced him to go. Jenna, having lost her own mother to cancer, and having faced the exact struggles this charity was helping, made it close to her heart.

Emeline didn't see Adam yet either when she arrived, and instead of hovering nervously at the entrance or sitting down at an empty table, she went straight upstairs to the bathroom. She had no idea why she was so nervous. Maybe it was because she hadn't gotten this dressed up in years, not since Rhonda and her husband had renewed their wedding vows three years ago. Perhaps her nerves were due to seeing Adam in a tux, even though he wore fancy tailored suits to work, or maybe she was terrified of seeing Sabine in his arms and what that would do to her.

She braced herself against the sink and took a few deep breaths. Better to just have fun tonight, and not overthink things. That's not what tonight was about. Taking a good look at herself in the mirror, the woman staring back at her was hardly recognizable, appearing almost otherworldly. Her hair was up in a loose chignon, dark liner and mascara with well blended gold tones on the lids to accentuate her eyes, a light blush, and glossy lips the color of caramel. The dress she wore may as well have been a piece of art. Sure, she loved to shop every once in a while, but there had never been an article of clothing she couldn't walk away from if it was too pricey, never an item she had dreamed of if it had gone out of stock or they didn't have it in her size—but this dress, when she saw it in a window, she knew she would not leave the cute little boutique store without it, twelve-hundred-dollar price tag be damned. It felt like a second skin when she had tried on the white and gold spaghetti-strapped dress. The plunge down the center between her cleavage may have been a little risqué, but it was too classy, too sexy, to be considered anything but. The belt around the torso looked like a gold ring encircling her, shiny to match the gold on the dress, and the bottom half fell in elegant flowy layers almost down to the floor. Thank goodness for her four-and-a-half-inch heels, which were white with gold trim to match.

She actually smiled at her reflection.

The door to the bathroom opened, and in walked Melody with a disgruntled Sabine behind her. "I'm sitting at your table, too," Melody said to her.

As if finally noticing Emeline, both women stopped talking and paused in their tracks. Emeline cleared her throat. "Is there a problem with the seating arrangement?"

"Who are you again?" Sabine asked dismissively.

Melody answered for her. "This is Emeline Bell, head of marketing." She turned to Emeline and smiled before adding, "She works very closely with Adam. That dress is simply stunning, by the way."

Melody was really starting to grow on Emeline now, and she would give her leave to *bup bup* any time she liked. "Thank you, Melody. You look lovely as always." Even though Sabine looked absolutely gorgeous in her black lace dress, the nude layer underneath making it appear as if the lace was covering up the naughty bits, Emeline didn't acknowledge it.

Melody actually blushed. "Well, you know." She waved a hand in the air. "We should definitely go shopping one day. Throw in a spa treatment and make it a whole shebang."

Whether the invitation was sincere, or just something to say, Emeline was about to respond that that sounded nice, when Sabine rudely interrupted.

"You two can have your little bonding moment later. There is a more pressing matter at hand." She looked straight at Emeline when she said, "Fix it."

"Fix what exactly?" She didn't care for her tone. She may be a supermodel, and she may be used to getting anything she wanted, but Emeline wasn't her little lap dog.

"The seating arrangement."

Emeline arched a brow. "What's wrong with it?"

"I'm supposed to be sitting with Adam." Her lips curled into a smug smile. "He is my date after all." The bitch knew she had dug into her. "Or didn't he tell you?"

Emeline's heart beat rapidly in her chest and she could almost feel the nausea setting in, but she would not let miss uppity see it. "As Melody already pointed out, I'm head of marketing, not Adam's personal life, and as far as the seating, I had nothing to do with the arrangement of that, so I'm afraid I can't help you. If you'll excuse me." She spared Melody, who looked sympathetic, a quick nod before she left the bathroom.

She had to lean against the wall as soon as the door shut and then she took a few calming breaths and stood there for as long as she could, for as long as she deemed it safe, before Sabine could open the door and find her standing there looking dejected.

No matter. It wasn't as if she had confessed her feelings to Adam, but she suddenly found herself thinking that he deserved way better than a manipulative, self-absorbed bitch, even if she did model sexy as sin lingerie.

She pushed off the wall and headed for the staircase. About halfway down the grand staircase, she locked gazes with a sharply dressed Adam. He wore a classic black and white tux, bow tie included, and his hair was pulled back in a ponytail at the base of his neck. He was such a stunning man, and yet he never seemed to acknowledge it, never really paid attention to women who constantly ogled him, making Emeline wonder if he was oblivious to it. She needed another intake of breath before proceeding down the rest of the steps.

He met her at the bottom and took her hand when she took the last step. She watched him swallow hard. "You look absolutely beautiful," he said, and then he kissed her once on each cheek.

Still, she could scarcely breathe let alone speak, but she managed to give him a slight smile, as much as the nervous muscles in her face would allow.

Adam let go of her hand and held out his arm. "Shall we?"

She was about to accept, when she heard Sabine call out Adam's name from the top of the stairs.

"There you are," she said as she sauntered down, Melody not far behind.

"Bup bup! Where do you think you're going with

that?" Melody called out to the two men carrying an ice sculpture. Even in stilettos, that woman walked incredibly fast, easily passing Sabine on the stairs without even holding on to the railing, and then in no time, she was steering the men and the ice sculpture into the great hall.

Finally, Sabine came over to where Emeline and Adam stood. He dropped the arm he had held out to Emeline.

"Can you believe this incredible mix-up?"

"What mix-up?" He arched a brow.

"We're not sitting at the same table," Sabine said as if that should have been obvious. "I'm going to see about changing that and then we can dance the night away so this evening won't drag."

By now Emeline had learned to tell, even with his subtlety, when Adam was upset about something. She noticed the tension in his jaw and the way his eyes slightly squinted. This night was important to him, and Sabine had callously made it about her. Just another evening to play dress up and concern herself with seating arrangements.

When Adam told Sabine there was no mix-up, Emeline stepped closer to him and curled her hand through his previously proffered arm. She could feel Adam's gaze boring into her while she addressed Sabine. "I'm afraid Adam's dance card is full tonight, Sabine." *That's right.* She'd just claimed him right in front of her.

Sabine glared at her before turning her attention to Adam. "I see," was all she said before she walked away and into the great hall.

She chanced a tentative glance at Adam whom she found smirking, looking completely amused. "Someone had to save you from her," she said sheepishly.

"My hero."

She shrugged. "I hope she at least brought her checkbook."

Adam chuckled at that, and then he led them both inside. When they reached their table, he pulled out her chair for her and then sat beside her. DeAnne and Christina joined them shortly after with their dates, followed by Rhonda, and then Joe, completing their table. There was one vacant chair since Joe had ordered the plus one, at the time thinking that there was a chance Jenna would be able to accompany him.

"All of you ladies better be prepared to take me for a spin, tonight," Joe told them when he sat down.

"What, I don't get the same invitation?" Adam joked.

If anyone at the table was shocked at Adam's joking demeanor, they covered it well. Joe laughed at the comment and then said, "Since you sign my paychecks, boss, I'll even let you twirl me."

Emeline's team had been getting used to Adam's presence at lunch, and after several outings, they even seemed to relax around him a bit more. She found it funny that for some reason, he had always been just Adam to her. From boorish, to friendly, she had always treated him as an equal, never shied away from speaking openly as she would to anyone else, although, she had never revealed so much of herself to anyone else.

"What is it?" Adam asked her, and that's when she realized she had just been caught staring.

She shook her head, indicating that it was nothing, but she knew he did not miss the blush she currently felt staining her cheeks.

He leaned in to whisper in her ear. "I believe your dance card is full tonight, Emeline, but I'll agree to part with you for one dance with Joe."

She swallowed hard and her pulse raced, both from the feeling of his nearness and the fact that he just, though unofficially, became her date for the evening. She caught Sabine's glare from across the room and held it with one of her own. She knew it was petty, but she felt protective over the man sitting next to her. He seemed annoyed and disinterested, and after what he did for her with Jarod, this was the least she could do for him. Not to mention the fact she was in love with him and had no desire to share him with the catty bitch.

Emeline had a feeling that sitting next to Adam all night or being held in his arms as they danced, would ensure that her heart rate would not return to complete normalcy this evening. However, now that she was somewhat stable, she was able to take in the full view of the ballroom. More than two dozen round tables were situated around the room with nearly three hundred people in attendance. Three large ice sculptures, including the one Melody had chased down, were in the shape of abstract art and situated in the center of a long table in the back. Pyramids of wineglasses were stacked on either side of the sculptures, and currently they were being filled. The dance floor was at the front of the room followed by the stage, where soft Jazz music was now being played. Waiters were coming around with champagne-filled flutes and fancy hors d'oeuvres, not a pig in a blanket in sight. Her stomach may have been tied in nervous knots, but no way was she about to miss out on mini servings of Beef Wellington and salmon tartare.

After the appetizers and the first course of salad were all served, it was time for Adam to take the stage and talk about his charity, Cancer Families. She squeezed his hand in encouragement, knowing how much he hated being the center of attention.

"Cancer is like an unwanted guest," he began

when he got up on stage, "insinuating itself into countless lives and definitely overstaying its welcome. I don't need a show of hands, because I know that when I ask how many of you have either suffered from cancer or know someone close to you who has, most, if not all of you, would raise your hands."

Emeline saw the emphatic nods go around the room.

"Those of you who wouldn't raise your hands, you fear it. And those of you who would have, fear it will come back. Cancer ravages the mind and body, it incites fear, and then it leaves devastation behind."

He may not have liked speaking in public, but Emeline observed that he was quite good at it. He wasn't making some speech written for him. He was speaking from the heart, causing Emeline's own heart to constrict. The crowd sat silently, riveted.

"I believe, that no matter your financial position in life, you should have every opportunity, the *same* opportunity, as everyone else to fight it. Because it is a fight. You're fighting for your life, and your family is fighting right there beside you. No one should have to worry about not being able to afford their medical care, or of not being able to pay their mortgage, or to put food on the table during that trying time. Isn't cancer enough of a fallout?"

Adam paused and took a deep breath. "My mother…" His voice broke. He cleared his throat, schooled his features, and began again. "My mother and father first started this charity more than twenty years ago. They wanted families to have one less burden to deal with. So, I thank you all for being here, and I ask you all to be generous when opening up your checkbooks tonight. Until there is a cure and the world is finally rid of cancer, what we do will never quite be enough, but at least we would have done something. Thank you."

The room erupted in applause, and Emeline noticed that she was hardly the only one wiping away some stray tears. When Adam returned to his seat, Emeline took his hand and held it under the table until the next course arrived.

The somber mood brightened a little as the evening went on. Their table was filled with good conversation, announcements were made every once in a while, indicating how much had been raised so far, and Joe, in Joe fashion, had been asking as many women to dance with him as possible. He wasn't a great dancer, but he looked like he had a blast.

Adam finally stood at one point and held his hand out for her. She placed hers in the palm of his, and he led her to the center of the dance floor where they could just disappear into the crowd. The song was a slow, jazzy beat and he held her closely, one hand around her waist, and one hand holding hers close to his chest, their gazes locked together. Somewhere in the middle of the song, Emeline wrapped her arms around his neck and he brought her even closer when he encircled her waist. She could feel the hard lines of his muscles pressed up against her. Her breasts felt heavy, aching for his touch, aching even more to feel his naked skin against them.

When the song ended, he surprised her by dipping her, and then he planted a gentle kiss on her forehead, making her wonder what those soft lips would feel like against hers or on other parts of her body.

She didn't dance to every song, but those she did, as promised, were danced with him, save for the one she promised Joe, and the two fast ones she danced with her girls *and* Joe, of course. The other men at their table had expressed how much they enjoyed the view.

"But Joe looked the sexiest," Rhonda's husband

remarked.

As the evening wound down, the guests began to slowly disperse. Sabine had not approached Adam again, not even to say goodbye before she left. Overall, the charity had raised quite a bit, and surprised gasps rang around the room when it was announced by the MC that Adam would be matching the donation.

"Did you drive here?" Adam asked her when it was time to go.

"I took a cab."

"I'll take you home," he said. He offered her his arm again on the way out.

A limo was waiting for them outside. Adam shrugged after he opened the door. "It's not every day you go to a ball." He gestured for her to get in, helping her with her dress, and then he slid in next to her after giving the driver her address.

"You're a good dancer," he told her.

"Not so bad yourself." She smiled. "My father taught me when I was little. He and my mom always used to dance around the house and they wanted to include me."

"Your eyes always light up when you talk about your parents," he said quietly before turning to face forward.

"And yours are always sad when you are trying to avoid talking about yours."

He didn't respond and the silence stretched between them as he seemed to be turning something over in his mind. Then finally, he spoke. "I accept your resignation."

She was so not expecting that. "You're firing me?"

"Of course not," he replied adamantly, finally turning to face her. "I meant what I said before. You're very valuable to this company and you've more than proven it. I also meant it when I told you that you would do great on your own. I don't want you to leave." He took her hand in his. "I want nothing more than for you stay, but I don't want to hold you hostage. That was unfair of me. Please, forgive me."

The truth was, she had forgotten about his threat. With the way he turned the company around along with giving her his friendship, not to mention the fact that she was in love with him, she was happy there again. She hadn't thought about quitting or about going out on her own. The fact that he remembered and was apologizing for it and even willing to let her go without any repercussions stunned her. She had already forgiven him a while ago.

She watched a sly smile form on his lips, a devilish gleam in his eye. "No one should have to work for an asshole."

"Good thing I no longer think of you as an asshole." She glanced down at their joined hands. "I would like to stay."

"You would?" He sounded surprised, hopeful even, and the look on his face confirmed it when she raised her head.

"And what about you, Adam?" she asked. "Do you intend to stay?" She knew it was a premature question, given the fact that it would be some time before he could present a tempting sale, but she felt like she needed to know if he even considered the possibility of actually keeping the company and running it himself.

He reached out and toyed with a strand of her hair. "I'd gotten so used to working with soulless corporations, people who wouldn't hesitate to stab each other in the back. I guess you can say I'm pleasantly surprised. Publishing Enchanted is more than a company.

It's a family."

"You're part of it now."

"And I don't think I want to give that up." He let go of her hair and brushed his knuckles down her cheek. "I have too many reasons to stay."

They were so close now, their faces mere inches apart. Emeline couldn't even remember how they had gotten there, but now she only wanted to be closer. "Adam," she whispered, right before he closed the final distance between them and kissed her.

His kiss was soft, tentative at first, as if gauging her reaction, but when she wrapped her arms around him, he deepened it, moaning into her mouth as their tongues finally met and entwined. Finally, she got her wish and fisted her hand in his thick locks. His hair was soft, just as she'd imagined. Even his beard was soft against her skin. And God, he was such a great kisser, exploring her mouth thoroughly, lips and tongues feverishly connecting.

It was her turn to moan when he pulled her onto his lap and his hands began to roam down her back, her arms, and skimming down the sides of her breasts. He stopped kissing her lips long enough to move down to her jaw, her neck, and then all the way down to that deep V in the center of her cleavage, eliciting another, much louder, moan from her.

She was so lost in him, she hadn't even realized at first that they were no longer moving, had no idea when they had stopped. Adam took notice of it, too, and paused his attentions to her. They were both panting as they stared at one another, and this time it was Emeline who leaned in and kissed him. She whispered, "Stay," against his lips, the ache inside her for him too great to be able to part with him.

He practically growled in response and the two of

them poured months of longing into their next kiss.

"I'm going to devour every single inch of you," he said.

Yes, please!

Chapter Thirteen

Emeline fumbled for her keys in her gold clutch while Adam was telling the limo driver to go, but he practically snatched the keys from her and opened the door to the lobby. She didn't miss the fact that his hands were shaking. She spared the night doorman a quick wave as she and Adam, hand in hand, practically sprinted through the lobby toward the elevators.

As soon as the elevator door slid open, he pulled her to him and fused his lips to hers again, walking her backwards inside. His roaming hands were bolder now, cupping her breast with one hand and her ass with the other. She thought she may actually come just from him touching her. Then she realized once again they weren't moving.

With a giggle against his lips, she said, "You have to press nine."

"Oh, right." He pressed the button for her floor and then pushed her up against the wall.

She felt his hard length pressing against her and emboldened herself to slide her hand in between them. He groaned when her hand made contact and then ground himself into her hand, moaning in her mouth as they feverishly kissed.

"God, I've wanted you for so long, Emeline."

"I've wanted you, too," she breathed.

The doors slid open. He clasped her hand in his and together they briskly walked the few feet it took to get to her apartment. Once again, he was the one who opened her door. The moment they stepped inside and shut the door, their hands and lips were on each other once again. It was dark, but the lights from the street illuminated enough.

Her keys along with her clutch were thrown on

the floor. Toed off shoes came right before he hoisted her up to straddle his hips, carrying her toward her hallway.

"Closet," she said when he opened up the wrong door.

He cursed. "I'm going to take you in that damned closet!"

He didn't. He continued to her bedroom, which was open, and stopped right beside the bed in the center of the room, letting her slide down to stand. Her knees felt weak, but he supported her.

He cursed again when he couldn't get her belt open.

"There's a catch inside in the back." She turned around and then felt his fingers slide inside the belt.

"Good. It'd be a shame to rip this pretty dress."

It would, but she wanted it off as badly as he did. Fortunately, he found the catch and the belt snapped open and fell in a light clang on the floor. At least the zipper was easy enough to slide down. He did it slowly, lavishing kisses down the open trail, and then he slid the straps down her shoulders, and then the dress down her body, bending down to steady her as she stepped out of it.

He didn't touch her right away when he stood back up. She heard the ruffling of clothes behind her and when he turned her around to face him, he stood shirtless and she got her first look at his naked chest and washboard abs. There was a light scattering of blond hair on his chest. She reached out with both hands and placed them on his shoulders and then she glided them down slowly, exploring the hard muscle underneath. She looked up at him when her hand reached the button of his pants and found him staring intently at her, hungrily.

He leaned down to capture her mouth again. This time the kiss was slow and explorative as they shed the rest of their clothes, along with the pins in her hair and the tie in his. Her nipples felt like hard points pressed against his warm, naked body, making her shudder, his unsteady breaths matching her own.

Finally, he lifted her up again as he crawled onto her bed and then gently laid her down underneath him. He kissed her lips, her neck, and then her ear. "You're so fucking beautiful," he whispered. He trapped her hands above her head, as he began his slow descent down her body, delivering open-mouthed kisses down her jaw, to her neck, and then finally stopping at her breasts.

Emeline moaned loudly when Adam bit down on her nipple and then louder still when he laved away the sting. He then gifted her other breast with the same attention. He released her hands and traveled further down her body, kissing, nipping, licking as he went, until he reached her center, his soft beard adding an extra sensation.

Her body bowed when his mouth connected with the most private part of her and he was relentless, devouring her as he had her mouth. He teased her tight bundle of nerves with just the tip of his tongue before finally laving all around.

With one hand in his hair and the other fisting the sheets beside her, she rode out his torture, chasing her completion, his large hands holding her inner thighs steady. When he sucked hard on her clit, she screamed and moved her head from side to side, as her climax hit her with a force like she'd never felt before.

Adam moaned against her, licking and kissing until her legs stopped quivering. After one final, intimate kiss, he crawled back up her body and took her lips again. "You see how delicious you taste? Better than the sweetest honey."

Even his words set her on fire, and again, the

ache was stirring despite the amazing orgasm he had just given her with his talented tongue. And she did like the taste of herself, especially since it was mixed in with his taste, one she was already becoming addicted to.

He moved down to suck on each breast again, giving one of them a lick before coming back up to face her. "I don't want anything between us, baby," he murmured. "Are you on the pill?"

She was. She didn't want anything between them either. She'd give him all of herself. And she liked the endearment. After establishing that they were both clean, he entered her in one long stroke. A sharp intake of breath escaped her as she adjusted to his sheer length and thickness. She'd never been with anyone that big before.

"Fuck!" he groaned. "You're so tight. Jesus, you feel so good."

She needed him to move, that ache inside her growing stronger. She moaned continuously as he slowly thrust inside her. He was gentle, pushing in and pulling halfway out, their bodies sliding against one another, and in between kissing her, he'd gaze at her adoringly. Then his strokes, though still slow, became harder, going deeper every time, and hitting a spot inside that made her orgasm start building again. Excited butterflies kept fluttering in her stomach with every thrust. His arms around her, the feel of his hips grinding against and moving hers, the smell of his cologne, and the scent of his hair was like the epitome of euphoria.

Her hands roamed down his defined back until she reached the firm globes of his ass, pressing him even closer to her. She locked her ankles around him, encouraging him to go faster, and with a long groan he complied. He began to thrust hard and fast, shaking the bed in the process, while she held on tightly to him and took what he gave her.

Emeline hugged him tightly to her and buried her face in his neck as her orgasm crashed upon her. She called out his name over and over again, her voice muffled by his neck, as she rode out wave after wave of infinite pleasure.

And then he was coming, too. "Oh, fuck! Emeline. Ah!" He ground out his release, moaning loudly, shuddering against her.

If the first orgasm he gave her could be equated to earth-shattering, then the second one could have split apart the universe. They both shook in each other's arms, still connected, even after the spasms had stopped.

When Adam finally pulled out, he rolled onto his back, taking her with him to lie half on top of him, her head resting on his shoulder. He tilted her chin up so that their eyes could meet and gave her a satisfied smile, one that she could not help but return.

"Hi," she said.

"Hi." He tapped her on the nose with his finger.

It seemed that just like her, he wanted to remain connected somehow and couldn't stop touching her. While she played with the sparse hairs on his chest, he glided his hand up and down her arm.

"That was really ... um…"

"Something," he finished for her, and they both laughed.

She'd had no idea that that kind of *something* was even possible. Not that she'd never orgasmed before. She just never felt anything like what she had just felt with Adam and not just reaching the finish line, but the whole of being connected to him, even with just his touch. Every part of her came alive, the feeling nearly overwhelming her.

"I think I was doing it wrong before," she said with mirth.

Adam let out a booming laugh that shook both her and the bed. "Me too."

That made her very happy to hear. Perhaps they had simply needed to find one another to feel this way.

They talked a little more until she yawned and it became contagious, and together they fell into that stage between being half awake and half asleep. Emeline did manage to drag herself out of bed at one point to go clean up and use the facilities, and when she crawled back into bed, he opened up his arms for her and cradled her. She loved the fact that he was definitely a cuddler. She actually had never been with one before and it had been so long since she shared a bed with someone anyway, but she realized she liked being held by him very much.

When the nightmare came again that night, the sound of a baby crying in the dark, instead of waking up alone, or in a cemetery, she awoke to Adam softly cooing to her, letting her know that he was there. She fell back into a dreamless sleep after that.

Emeline awoke first, with her head on Adam's chest, her arm draped over his stomach, while his curled around her hip, and her left leg was draped over his thigh. The sound of his heart beating and even breathing was such a calming force. When she lifted her head, she found him sleeping peacefully, his face relaxed, and she couldn't help but reach out and touch his cheek and softly kiss his lips. His mouth twitched a little, but other than that, he didn't stir, so she decided to let him sleep in. Before she got out of bed though, she couldn't help steal a glance at his gloriously naked body, including his heavy and impressive appendage lying off to the side in semi-erectness.

About forty-five minutes later, she was showered and standing by the stove with her hair up in a messy bun, finishing up some scrambled eggs and bacon, wearing nothing but an…

"Holy baby Jesus, you can kill a man like that," Adam said from behind her.

She coyly glanced over her left shoulder, seeing him standing in nothing but his sexy boxer briefs, with his jaw dropped open. "You're in great shape." She giggled. "You can take it."

She wore nothing but an apron, her bare bottom fully on display for him. In seconds, he was at her back, playfully biting her neck and cupping her breasts, one of which was peeking out of the retro-looking apron, with its gray and white stripes, accented with bright orange clementines and green leaves and frills around the edges.

He continued to torment her with his tongue and teeth on the back of her neck, while his hands massaged her breasts and talented fingers plucked her straining nipples. When he let his hand roam further south and under the front of her apron, he inserted two fingers into her wetness. She spread her legs wider to give him more access and threw her head back against his chest, letting out a loud moan in the process.

"I think it's done," he said referring to breakfast.

He turned off the stove and twirled her around to face him. His lips caught hers, his tongue invaded, filling her senses with him, and then his fingers resumed their torture, only this time he reached her entrance by sliding his hand down her ass.

When he released her mouth, the look he wore was almost primal. It must have matched her own, she thought, because she felt ravenous for him.

Without a word, he removed his fingers and tugged her over to the table, turning her to face it as soon as they reached it. Fortunately, she hadn't set it yet, otherwise, if he didn't shove everything out of the way, she would have. With his hand on her back, he guided her forward. When her upper body lay flat on the table, he stretched her arms straight out in front of her and covered her body with his. She heard his harsh breathing as he delivered open-mouthed kisses to her, descending a trail down to her ass. He kissed each cheek and then made her giggle when he gently bit down on one.

"You have such an amazing ass," he remarked, right before he widened her stance and dove his tongue in between the center of her folds.

All laughter died right then, and she curled the hands in front of her into fists as he licked and sucked on her wanton flesh.

He stood abruptly and placed his body over hers again. "Like honey," he murmured in her ear right as he impaled her. She felt the material of his briefs against her until he slid them down further.

There was nothing gentle about their lovemaking this time, and she loved every second of him pounding into her. She let out loud keening sounds and successive moans unabashedly as he hit all the places that incited her. He went deeper still when he lifted off of her and placed his hands on her hips.

She loved how vocal he was as well, shouting out expletives in between his hard grunts. "I love the way you fucking feel," he called out, his voice gravelly, as he continued with his fast pace. He drove into her, taking her higher, to her peak. "Come for me, Emeline. I want to hear you scream my name again."

His was an easy request to comply with, what with her already there, fueled by not only his words, but her desire for him. Her orgasm hit her with an intense ferocity, crashing down on her in waves, and she took Adam with her. He stilled briefly and then continued his movement with a few slow, hard thrusts as he spilled inside her, and then he collapsed on top of her, supporting the bulk of his weight on his forearms on either side of her.

"I think you killed me."

"What a lovely way to go," he said nuzzling her neck. And then he was off of her, cleaning her up, looking suddenly intense. He seemed to be examining her. "I didn't hurt you, did I?"

She laughed, and saw his face lighten as well. She stood on her tiptoes and wrapped her arms around his neck and kissed him softly. "I loved last night, but I also loved just now." She felt her cheeks flush, though she didn't care. She wanted him to know how he made her feel. Whether they did it fast or slow, or with her bent over a table, all of it was amazing if it was with him. "I liked the intensity of that."

"You like it a little rough," he acknowledged. His smile was breathtaking, his gaze on her hungry again, and his touch as he brushed his knuckles down her cheek was tender.

She nodded.

Fortunately, their breakfast and coffees were still warm and though they started out eating side by side, he ended up pulling her from her chair and onto his lap, and the two of them finished eating while feeding each other and laughing.

She had no idea how she had the stamina to go again, but she did. They ended up on the couch after breakfast with her straddling him, on top.

"Leave it on," he ordered as she was about to remove her apron. "I like it." She watched his pupils darken, right before he inched up and licked one of her exposed breasts. "God, you have such beautiful tits, a glorious ass, and a pussy that tastes like honey. A man can write sonnets about your body alone."

Her mouth dropped open. "Oh my God! I can't

believe you just said that."

He let out a booming laugh at what she surmised must have been her shocked expression. Who knew her reserved Adam had it in him. He looked almost boyish in his carefree laughter, and it only endeared him more to her. That, and she had to admit she liked his complimentary vulgarity.

She didn't want to think about Sabine in this moment, but knowing he had been with someone who personified perfection into print, yet he was looking at *her* like the sun rose and set in her presence, warmed her heart. What they had between them felt bigger than surface level, and, at least for her, it ran soul deep.

She made his laughter die down when she bent forward, her hair a curtain around them, and kissed him with intense ferocity. He threaded his fingers in her hair and gave back everything she gave him. She lifted up, used her free hand to position him at her entrance, and then she slid all the way back down his length, heat unfurling in her lower belly.

They spent the whole day together, laughing, talking, exchanging mind-blowing orgasms. She'd never spent a day like that with anyone before. Neither of them broached the subject of the elephant in the room—what it would be like at work tomorrow. She thought perhaps, as with a lot of other things, they were on the same page. It was probably better to see how and where things progressed before announcing anything publicly, not to mention the fact that she kind of looked forward to the excitement of sneaking around.

There was also the one small fact that she was in love with him, and while she could absolutely see he cared for her, she had no idea if he loved her in return. The last thing she needed was everyone in the office to pity her crushed heart. If he was going to crush it, she'd rather suffer in silence.

Chapter Fourteen

"What?"

It hadn't even been five minutes since Emeline walked into work, before Rhonda, DeAnne, and Christina strolled into her office and closed the door behind them. She had been thinking about Adam's mouth on her breast this morning, waking her up better than any alarm clock ever did. He hadn't wanted to leave her last night, and she hadn't wanted him leave. To put them both out of their misery, she had suggested that he stay, and to show his acceptance and appreciation of her invitation, he had thrown her over his shoulder and carried her off to her bedroom where he had thanked her several times.

She couldn't remember dreaming at all last night, only feeling secure in the safety of Adam's arms.

In the morning, they reveled in each other again before he went home to shower and change. He had beaten her to the office, texting her that she was a slow poke, but she hadn't seen him yet.

"Don't you 'what' me," DeAnne said.

"Ease up on the poor girl," Rhonda said. "But seriously, you're glowing. That's a very good look on you."

So much for keeping things quiet, Emeline grumbled internally. "Look, it's all new still, and I don't—"

"Oh, please, it goes without saying that none of us will yap to anyone." DeAnne waved her hand dismissively in the air and sat herself down on the corner of Emeline's desk.

"You look happy, darlin'," Rhonda said.

"You really do," Christina added. "And I'm so happy for you."

"And you look really well f—"

"DeAnne!" Rhonda playfully smacked her friend on the shoulder, but all of them laughed.

"I think we all misjudged him at first," Rhonda began, "but I also think you had a lot to do with the changes around here. It seems like he'd do anything for you."

They had no idea just how much. "He's a good man. I misjudged him, too." And he had a lot to do with the change in her as well. She had fully opened up her closed off heart to someone after twenty years.

"After everything you've been through recently with Jarod, I think you deserve a little happiness," Christina said.

Emeline was touched by her concern.

After failing to pry out juicy details from her, the girls went back to work, but not before DeAnne got something else in. "You know, I've often fantasized about that meeting room desk, but sadly no one in the office ever really piqued my interest."

"DeAnne!" Rhonda, Christina, and Emeline, said in unison this time.

"Just sayin'."

Emeline shook her head and let out an exasperated breath at her friend's antics, although, the thought of him taking her on that table sent stabs of desire to her belly.

DeAnne left her office with a wink, followed by Rhonda. Christina stayed behind a few moments to deliver her messages and go over some of the agenda for today.

Emeline couldn't help herself. After Christina had left her office, her mind wandered again, thinking back to how much things had changed this weekend, and how incredibly difficult it was going to be to concentrate today, given the fact that simple thoughts of Adam were firing up her body as if they were livewires coming in contact with water.

****

Adam couldn't concentrate, and it was all Emeline's fault. He picked up the receiver and pushed the button to connect to Emeline's office. "I need to see you in my office, Ms. Bell," he said when she answered.

A minute later, she was at his door. After a few soft raps, she opened it without him telling her to enter, and she closed it behind her. "Ms. Bell?" She arched a sexy brow.

It had only been a few hours since he'd last seen her, but he already missed her—her face, her scent, the feel of her body melting in with his.

"Yes, *Ms. Bell*. I seem to have a hard time concentrating today."

She swallowed hard, and a beautiful blush stained her cheeks. She stood only feet away from him, but the distance may as well have been miles. "Why is that?" He heard her, though she spoke barely above a whisper.

"Because I keep thinking about you in that sexy little apron." And about her luscious naked body spread out before him, her moans as he made love to her, her rapturous facial expressions as she came for him with *his* name on her lips. He'd had sex plenty of times before, but he'd never made love to even a single woman. Whether he had Emeline bent over a table, underneath him, or writhing on top, all of it was making love. All of his pent-up emotional and physical feelings for her came crashing down on him, as if he even needed them to know how he felt about her, how he had begun to feel about her since the day they met. She was permanently branded under his skin, in his blood, and she was his.

He watched a coy smile appear on her face.

"Have you written sonnets about me yet?"

"Tons," he said. "And dirty limericks," he added with a chuckle. "I'll recite them for you one day." He had to adjust himself as her heated gaze bored into him.

"I look forward to hearing them." Another coy smile as she sauntered, yes sauntered, over to him. "Even the dirty limericks." She came to stand in between his legs. "Looks like you need some help concentrating."

She dropped down to her knees and freed him from the confines of his pants. "Oh, sweet Jesus!"

He had to stifle a moan as she took him in her mouth. Over and over, he watched her plump lips take his cock in as far as she could, her hand stroking the excess. She had gifted him with her sexy mouth over the weekend, but there was something so much more erotic with having her do it to him in the office. He could not recall how often he had pictured having her on his desk, and on every other surface of the office for that matter. He'd tuck those ideas away for later, but they would both need to be careful. He couldn't bear the thought of anyone thinking negatively about her, not her, especially not in a work environment she loved so much. There were already enough murmurings about Jarod, and he had a feeling she really didn't like attention any more than he did. He wasn't sure she would be receptive to any grand announcements yet.

What shocked him was how much *he* was ready. Adam felt like a caveman. He wanted to beat his chest and finally, after three grueling months of longing, claim the woman who was currently torturing him ever so sweetly. He threw his head back on his chair and made a low growling sound.

Instead of popping him out of her mouth when he warned her he was coming, she swallowed everything he gave her. She stood and leaned over him to kiss him.

"Couldn't stain your fancy pants, now could we?"

Adam laughed against her lips. "You're very considerate, and thorough, I might add. Thank you for that." He kissed her again, his tongue caressing hers, infusing more of his thanks into it.

"Think you can concentrate now?" she asked with an impish smile.

"Oh, baby, you just gave me a fantastic blowjob in my office, so now I'm going to be picturing you giving me one in that apron."

She smiled at him and sat on his lap, wrapping her arms around him. "I'll buy some more."

"Jesus, I'm going to buy you a store's worth of them for Christmas."

Emeline smiled wider at that, and he realized that maybe she understood, that even though it was still weeks away, he was making plans. He hated the idea of her doubting his intentions. And then her smile faded.

"What is it, Emeline?"

"My father and I are flying to Paris for Christmas. We take turns each year with Phillippe's family, and this year it's our turn."

"Oh, well, that sounds wonderful." He wondered if his voice sounded as disappointed as he felt at not being able to spend Christmas with her. He actually hadn't even thought about Christmas this year, but now that he had, he felt a lonely ache at not spending it with her. "How long will you be away?"

"Five days including the weekend. I had put in for a few personal days over the summer."

A short silence stretched between them until Emeline broke it. "Adam?" He watched her worry her lip for a few seconds. "Would you like to come with me?"

His eyes widened. "You want me to come spend Christmas with you and your family?"

She nodded, then shrugged her shoulders. "I think I'd miss you too much if you didn't."

It was Adam's turn to smile wide now. He mentally berated himself for not letting her know first that he would miss her. "I would miss you, too." He took hold of one of the hands she had wrapped around his neck and kissed her open palm. "Thank you, Emeline. I would love to come."

He hugged her, felt her heart beating against his. For so long, he had thought his heart was too cold to give to anyone, but Emeline had stolen it, breathed warmth into and awakened it. Whether she had meant to or not, the whole of his heart now belonged to her.

Chapter Fifteen

Adam hadn't really had a happy Christmas since he was a child. His father would often be working even on the eve and the day of, leaving him with the housekeeper and butler. There would always be presents, something his father's secretary had picked out, something thoughtless, but lavish and expensive, things he never really cared for, especially since he had no real friends to speak of to share them with.

His current situation, sitting coach on the plane to Paris, his half eaten, mostly flavorless dinner pushed aside, was neither lavish nor expensive, not by his standards anyway. Yet with Emeline asleep and snuggled up beside him, he had never felt more content. While his father's estate had come complete with a private jet, Adam did not want to push or boast about his fortune. He was a guest on this trip after all, and Emeline, as he had observed, was not one for overt extravagance, and neither was he for that matter. Strange, he thought, considering his upbringing. That did not mean, however, that Emeline's father was not currently graciously enjoying his seat up in first class. It was the only seat available on Emeline's flight for him to book on such short notice, and he happily gave it up to Edmund so he could sit next to his girl.

"Wake up, Princess," he whispered in her ear when the plane began to make its decent to Charles de Gaulle Airport. He knew the view looking out the window would be beautiful as the bright lights welcomed them, but he'd been to Paris before, and it paled in comparison to the view of sleepy, cognac eyes staring up at him. He kissed her lips. "Did you have a good sleep?"

Emeline looked a little surprised when she answered. "I did. I seem to be sleeping well quite a lot lately."

"Me too." He pulled her close and kissed the top of her head.

Phillipe was already waiting for them by the time they exited the airport. He hugged Emeline first before he kissed each cheek. "Pleasant flight?" he asked her in French. "You look very well."

He clapped Adam on the back, seemingly genuinely happy to see him, and Adam took his slight nod as appreciation for taking care of his cousin like he had promised him at the karaoke bar.

And finally, Phillipe hugged Edmund. "You look well, also, Uncle. You must really have enjoyed first class."

"I did." Edmund gave a slightly tipsy smile. "The scotch was exquisite."

Adam made a mental note that perhaps the next trip, he would book in advance and have all three of them seated in first class. Maybe he'd even try to sneak in a trip on his private jet after all at some point, given how much Edmund seemed to enjoy the flight. As he helped Phillipe load the suitcases into the trunk, he realized that he'd just been planning for the future, something he'd been doing an awful lot lately. And the funny thing was, that it wasn't even scaring the shit out of him.

Emeline's family had welcomed him warmly when they arrived. It was a small party at the house, consisting of Philippe and his mother, Claudette—his father was nowhere in sight—and his mother's sister Nicolette, with her college-aged daughter, Simone. The four-bedroom house was tucked snugly among a few tall trees, with a well-kept garden—a charming mix of old school meeting modern. The interior was a mirror of the outside with its antique feel mixed with some contemporary renovations, particularly the kitchen with its stainless-steel appliances. It was Philippe's childhood home, which he, his mother, aunt, and cousin lived in.

Though Adam and Emeline never officially declared their status, her family kept referring to him as her boyfriend. Perhaps she had referred to him that way when she informed them she was bringing him, but it didn't matter the way his title came about. All he knew was that he liked it, and he noticed Emeline's blush and smile and figured she liked the sound of it, too.

He had to admit that the sneaking around at work had been fun these past couple of weeks, but being able to hold her hand in public, brush away a strand of hair from her face, or even kiss her on the cheek had been liberating. It felt natural.

Rightness. It kept washing over him. With Emeline especially, but also with work lately. He was no longer the unapproachable boss or some guy who came in to simply shake up a company. No, he belonged there, and instead of fear, he found himself garnering respect.

As the party sat down to dinner the next night on Christmas Eve, a sense of family washed over him, even though they were not his family. He looked over at Emeline, wrapped in easy conversation with her cousins, and a warmth settled over him.

They were not his family … yet.

****

For the first time since his mother was alive, Adam actually felt like a kid on Christmas morning. He tore the wrapping off Emeline's present with gusto and was touched to see something thoughtful from her. Fancy name plates custom made for him for both his office door and desk, something he hadn't yet bothered to do. She also gave him a gag gift—a mug that read "World's Greatest Boss" and then she whispered in his ear, "I have something else to give you later."

He whispered back, "Me too, but for now…" He handed her a box, hoping like mad she would like his gift.

"Oh, Adam. These are beautiful."

He had gotten her jewelry, a matching set comprised of dangly earrings, a necklace, and a bracelet. The stones embedded in each item were the color of cognac. "It was as close as I could get to match the color of your eyes."

"So beautiful," Nicolette said as she came over to get a closer look. She then picked up Adam's mug and read the writing aloud in English. "You are lucky, Emeline. My boss would get a mug that said world's biggest piece of *merde*."

The room erupted in laughter, while he and Emeline both tried to stifle theirs. No doubt she was recalling the rough start to their own working relationship.

"And my boss certainly does not look like your Adam here," she went on before muttering something under her breath in French about her boss's pinched nose and poor hygiene.

Later, when they were both alone in the bedroom no one had batted an eye to them sharing, they both laughed as they exchanged their private gifts. She had bought several more aprons, despite not really being much of a cook, but they had another purpose, after all, and he had bought her some as well, thereby pretty much making good on his threat of stocking aprons for her to the brim. They were all sexy, in much the same frilly fashion as the first one she had worn for him, but all different designs, all in skimpy retro fashion prints, pinstripes, plaids, and even one that looked like an old-fashioned maid would wear.

"I think you and I have a bit of a twisted fetish

going on here," she remarked.

It was one that he was more than happy to explore further. "I can't go five entire days without ravishing your sweet little cunt."

"Adam!" She feigned shock, as she often did, used to his "sexy", as she'd put it, vulgarity by now. She pointed out that they were in a house full of people, though her protest contradicted the desire he saw in her eyes.

"We'll be very quiet."

Emeline snorted. And then with a quiet vulnerability, she admitted that the orgasms he gave her often made her feel as if the world were about to split in two. Adam often felt the very same thing.

"Quiet and sex with my handsome beast of a man are definitely not synonymous," she added with a chuckle.

He loved her use of the word, "my" in that sentence, for she was definitely his. His mouth descended on hers with fierce longing, and it seemed her caution flew out of the window. "Put this one on," he ordered, holding up a slightly see-through lace apron. He quickly helped her undress, before shedding his own clothes in record time. His breaths came out heavy beside her as his hands collided with her bare skin.

He helped her with the ties of the apron as she sat with her back to him, her legs tucked underneath her, giving him a glorious view of part of her ass. His saucy little beauty was breathtaking.

Emeline shivered and moaned in his arms as they encircled her, bringing her flush against his chest. She ground into his hard length pressing against her. He had to still her movements, lest he finish before he even got started. When she tilted her head back for a kiss, he happily obliged, fueling it with fire and longing.

When their kiss ended, she turned in his arms to face him and maneuvered herself to straddle him. Adam adjusted himself as well, sitting on his haunches so he'd be able to move easily with her. They kissed again, as if on instinct to be connected. Slower this time, tongues twining exploratively, with gentle bites to each other's lips in between. When their hands began to roam freely, it was all Adam could take. He had reached his breaking point and needed to be inside her. He grabbed her ass and lifted her up and then onto his straining cock, and all the while he never broke their kiss. He set a steady pace, pushing up into her as she ground down against him.

He kissed her lips sweetly and then delivered one final nip to her bottom lip before proceeding to lavish open-mouthed kisses down her neck and all the way down to a taut nipple peeking out of her new apron. He laved his tongue around it before sucking the hard peak into his mouth, making his girl shiver once again. She moaned softly, and he knew that she was struggling to be as quiet as possible, just like he was.

He gazed up at her, meeting her eyes, as he continued to torment her breast. She looked at him, her face the picture of ecstasy, eyes hooded and darkened with desire. When she bit down on her lip again, that became his undoing.

He took her mouth in another fiery kiss as he adjusted their positions once again. Supporting her back, he sat up with her and laid her down on the bed, him flush against her, and he quickened his pace. Chasing after both of their orgasms, which were right at the precipice, he delivered long, hard strokes.

"You look so fucking beautiful underneath me like that," he said, his voice gruff.

Her reply was an incoherent sound, but the way she tenderly brushed her fingers down his cheek and the way she looked at him spoke volumes.

This was what love looked like.

He swallowed her moans with another earth-shattering kiss as she fell apart in her arms, his own climax hitting him barely seconds later with the force of a freight train. When his spasms subsided, he stayed connected to her, burying his face in her neck. He loved the way she ran her fingers through his now disheveled locks. It made him feel cherished.

Eventually, they managed to disentangle themselves long enough to clean up. Most of which was a blur, from the getting up to falling back to bed and snuggling Emeline in his arms. What he did recall with great clarity was the feeling of being completely content as they held onto each other before he fell asleep.

Chapter Sixteen

Valentine's Day was two weeks away, and Adam felt like a sappy fool. He needed to call the whole thing off. He realized he hadn't even said the words to her out loud yet. Had she, for that matter? She had to know he loved her. He could feel her love for him pouring through every time they made love, or kissed, or simply the way she would gaze at him adoringly. Perhaps, the words were more difficult for both of them to say than for most. They had both been so closed off, and for so long, it had been their common fear.

He walked over to his office window and gazed out on the darkening sky. The snow was still falling, though not nearly as bad as the blizzard they'd had last week. New York City in the winter time, though sometimes a pain in the ass for travel, was breathtaking. The snow was like a white blanket on the ground, on cars, on trees. It gave the normally bustling city a serene appearance. Things just seemed to quiet down then.

The first snowfall of the season came the day he and Emeline had returned from their trip to Paris. Something had shifted for them after that. Their behavior in the office was still reserved, though he knew that Emeline's team were aware of their relationship. If she hadn't already confirmed his suspicions, then DeAnne giggling like a loon around him would have. Most everyone else, however, either suspected, didn't know, or pretended like they didn't know. Either way, work was work, and he and Emeline continued to do their jobs, side by side, steering the publishing company forward in wonderful new directions. The café was a complete success, and plans were underway for several more. The website was also doing well and had brought in exponential sales already. Adam was confident that in a few years' time their little boutique publishing house may even rival some of the bigger fish.

The moments he and Emeline had spent out of the office were amazing as well. From trying to teach her the impossible—ice-skating—and failing miserably, to quiet evenings at one of their apartments, to dinners, to talking, to ravishing each other's bodies, and even in the office, sneaking around exploring a few sexual fantasies. There was no doubt in his mind that this was the woman he wanted forever with.

So why was he going to allow the damn ring in his pocket to burn a hole for another two weeks? Because he was a sappy fool. He wanted a story to tell his kids about how he proposed to their mother in a restaurant with violins playing. He was pretty sure Emeline would say yes, or rather, he hoped like hell she would, but she'd laugh about it later. It wasn't her style. It wasn't his style either. He wanted to call the restaurant and cancel the damned reservation. Instead, he should plan something quiet and romantic at home with just the two of them.

His cell phone buzzed in his back pocket snapping him out of his reverie. It was a text from Emeline. "Mr. Charmont, I need to see you in the meeting room."

Everyone else had gone for the night, but Emeline had drawn all the blinds in the meeting room closed. She had been tormenting him with her sexy little black and white dress all day. The front of it, though sewn to the dress, looked a bit like an apron. She'd sat in this very room with him earlier while he conducted a meeting, with a knowing, tempting little smile.

"You're lucky I didn't bend you over that table in front of everyone earlier," he said as he walked into the meeting room. He shut the door behind him.

She was casually leaning against the head of the

table, the chair moved out of the way, and all thoughts about Valentine's Day and the ring were put aside. He'd figure out the right moment eventually, but for now he just wanted her. He was already painfully straining against his zipper.

He strode up to her with purpose, a predator about to catch his prey, and fused their lips together, and then he entwined his tongue with hers, tasting her delicious flavor. He reveled in her moans as he sucked her bottom lip into his mouth. He'd never get enough of her taste or the feel of her.

He cursed when he slid a hand up her thigh and reached her apex to find her without any panties.

"I took them off," she replied breathlessly.

He lifted her dress and almost came at the sight of her nearly bare pussy and thigh-high stockings held by a garter belt. He dropped to his knees and dove in to taste her honey. He used his thumbs to spread her lips, giving him better access to lick and suck her more sensitive areas, and he was rewarded with her loud moans of appreciation. As much as he wanted to keep feasting on her delicious flavor though, he found himself too close to the edge.

He stood, and in a few quick and graceful moves, he turned her and had her bent over the table with her ass on display for him.

"Hurry, Adam," she pleaded with desperation in her voice. She was just as needy for him as he was for her, it seemed.

As soon as he sprang free, he entered her and immediately set a punishing pace, pounding into her while holding onto her hip with one hand and bracing himself against the table with the other, flesh slapping against flesh. It wasn't enough right now. He needed her mouth. Before she had time to protest him pulling out of her, he flipped her around again and hoisted her up so that her ass was on the table and he quickly impaled her again.

She wrapped her legs around his hips, her arms around his neck, and their lips met fervently. He let his hands roam everywhere he could reach, her back, her neck, her thighs, and then he threaded one of them in her hair.

God, how he loved the feel of her.

And then he felt her tightening around him, like a warm, velvet vise, and he knew she was close. Good, he thought, because he was right there at the edge with her.

"Scream my name, baby," he commanded against her lips.

He slowed down to deliver hard, deep strokes, burying his face in her neck. When he gently nipped her there, she came, calling out for him, clutching him as spasms rocked her body. He came with her, saying her name as if she were a prayer on his lips.

They stayed like that for a while, clinging to each other.

Adam found it interesting how even when their foreplay started out playfully, they always seemed to end on an intense note. Being with her felt intense, and coming in her, with her, often shattered him.

"Take me home," she said after they cleaned up.

He only hoped that soon, those words would come to mean something else—going home to a place they both shared.

Chapter Seventeen

"Are you all right?" Christina asked her the next morning when she followed her into her office.

"Yeah, why do you ask?"

"You seem like you have something on your mind."

She did actually. Yesterday, her late-night office tryst had fulfilled a huge fantasy, one that she was definitely not sharing, especially with DeAnne. She'd never hear the end of it from that woman about how it was her idea to do it in the conference room. Besides, it was a private moment between her and Adam. After she and Adam had had dinner, they showered together and made love slowly. They had seemed more connected than ever, but this morning he had been acting a bit strange. Something fell out of his pocket when his jacket slipped off the chair he had draped it over the night before, and he sprinted for it, telling her it was nothing important when she had asked him what it was, and then he had left her apartment in a rush after a quick peck on the lips.

"I'm fine, really," she assured Christina.

By the look on her assistant's face, she wasn't buying it, but she did go back to her desk to get started on today's projects.

A few hours later, Emeline went into Adam's office to go over the latest numbers with him, and he was back to his usual self with her, as if the morning was forgotten. She decided to stop overthinking things and just let it go. Maybe it really was nothing. She'd much rather focus on the amazing night they'd had instead.

She went back to her office with a smile on her face, but she realized she had forgotten something.

"Yes?" Adam answered when she rang his office.

He had drawled out the word, making her giggle.

"I'm heading out to lunch in a few. Want to join?"

"Why, what would the neighbors think?" This time he put on a thick Texan accent, which he was quite good at, making her give a full-on belly laugh this time.

Finally, when her laughter subsided, she replied, "It's a group outing, so your virtue will be safe."

"I'd love to, Princess," he said, dropping the southern accent, "but I have a conference call with Melody and a possible investor in fifteen minutes."

"Want me to bring you back something?"

"Sure, surprise me." He then added, "You know what I like," suggestively.

Emeline definitely knew what she liked as well and decided that maybe she'd let him have her for lunch later, too.

As she was about to head out with the girls and Joe, a messenger arrived wearing a silly Cupid costume. He wore a golden, short, curly wig, make-up that would befit a mime, and a red and white onesie with wings attached. He also came complete with a bow and arrow slung off his shoulder, and he was carrying what appeared to be a stack of rag magazines. He stopped at Christina's desk, and by then the messenger had the attention of practically everyone in the office, even Adam popping his head out to see what all the fuss was about.

At first, Emeline thought that maybe Adam had something to do with this, that somehow, he'd decided to go public with their relationship, despite his earlier joke about the neighbors. Perhaps he'd done that to throw her off. The truth was, that mostly everyone in the office probably already knew by now anyway. They weren't physical other than behind closed doors, but sometimes, just by the endearing way he'd speak to her in front of others before he'd realize his folly and switch to professional mode, may have been a dead giveaway. She was certain that she herself had been guilty of that at times.

Furthering her suspicion, the messenger asked for Emeline.

"That's me," she said and then her gaze locked with Adam's. She half expected him to be smiling, or doing something to acknowledge this was his doing, but he seemed puzzled, and began to walk toward her.

Cupid said nothing to her at first. Instead, he walked around the room randomly passing out the magazines to people, saving the last one in his hand for her.

She didn't understand what she was looking at right away. It was a series of photographs of Adam and Sabine stepping out of his lobby, the two of them embracing, Adam opening the door of a cab for her. The title read "Midnight Tryst: Sabine and Her Boy Toy at It Again." These were taken the day before yesterday. Adam hadn't slept over that night.

She looked up in time to see Adam snatch the rag from someone. She could feel everyone staring at the two of them. When Adam looked up at her, his eyes were pleading. She was about to go back into her office, she hoped with Adam in tow to explain, when she remembered the idiot who had just purposefully strolled in here to hand out these rags to her and her coworkers. She was fuming.

"Who the fuck sent you to give these to *me*?" Emeline demanded.

"I'm really sorry about this," the guy replied, though he hardly looked sorry at all. And he wasn't finished with her yet, it seemed. "I'll lose my job if I don't deliver this message."

Emeline was about to protest. She didn't want to hear it. Somewhere in the back of her mind, she knew who was responsible, but the bastard Cupid took out a harmonica and began to play out of tune. "Whore!" he yelled, followed by something about karma coming to bite her in the ass, but the guy never had a chance to finish, since Adam grabbed him by the scruff, and then their new in-office burly security guard was tossing him out.

Meanwhile, Rhonda began going around the room, collecting all the magazines, and then DeAnne and Christina joined in helping her, all the while Emeline stood frozen as her world came crashing down on her. Jarod, it seemed, wasn't done with her, and now Adam, who she once again recalled acting weird this morning, may or may not be hooking up with his ex.

"Don't look at me like that, Emeline," Adam practically yelled, startling her out of her paralyzed state with his unexpected outburst. He fisted the magazine. "This is garbage. I'm with you, not with her. Did you get all that?" he added, addressing the room.

Well, that was definitely *a* way of making their relationship public. Wordlessly, she turned on her heel and went to her office, slamming the door behind her.

Seconds later, Adam walked in. He was angry, but so was she, not to mention embarrassed, and scared if it was in fact Jarod who orchestrated this, although, it occurred to her that it may also gave been Sabine.

"Emeline, I need to explain."

"Yes, you do. You fucking do!" She took a deep breath, because the last thing she needed right now was a screaming match for everyone in the office to be privy to. "But I was just humiliated in front of my coworkers. Called a whore by a man waving around pictures of my boyfriend with another woman. A boyfriend who decided *that* was the right time to announce that we were a couple, and all of this was most likely orchestrated by my psychotic stalker. I need a few minutes here."

His features contorted into both shock and anger now, as if just realizing that Jarod may have had something to do with this. He took a step toward her, but she held up her hand to stop him.

"Please don't," she whispered. If he hugged her now, she'd lose it. Maybe she should have known that these past few months of happiness were all she was going to get.

Adam nodded. The sting of her rejection was evident in his eyes, but she felt too numb to care right now, to numb to even cry. He left her office, shutting the door softly behind him.

Suddenly, she felt like the walls were closing in on her and she couldn't stay here another minute. She walked out, told Christina she was going home early today, and though she felt everyone watching her, she didn't spare a glance for anyone else. She was grateful that at least the girls knew when to give her space and she knew they'd be there if she needed them.

Emeline couldn't even recall how she got home, acting solely on autopilot, but when she did, when she was away from prying eyes, and finally alone, she let heart-wrenching sobs consume her while she got undressed, while she sat on the floor of the tub as the water from the showerhead washed over her, and even as the water ran cold, until she had no more tears left to cry. Still, she felt numb. When she finally emerged from the bathroom, her hair dripping and wearing a thin robe that left her shivering, she heard the loud banging on her door.

It was Adam. He walked right past her when she

opened it.

"Come right on in," she said sarcastically.

He walked into the living room, and she followed, though she stopped several feet away from him. His eyes widened when he turned to face her, surely seeing the after effects of her crying, and he made as if to reach out for her, but then pulled back.

"She came to see me the other day," he said, his voice hoarse.

"Why didn't you tell me then?" Emeline asked accusingly.

"Because it wasn't important," he snapped. "I had other things on my mind." He threw his hands up. "She showed up on my doorstep, her usual style whenever she's in town. She literally was in my apartment for a whole of ten bloody minutes. I told her I had a steady girlfriend now, that *you* were my girlfriend. I also made it very clear to her that that part of our relationship was over. I actually thought I had made it clear to her the last time she was here. I called a taxi for her and walked her downstairs. That was it. She gave me a hug goodbye, because I think she actually may have gotten it this time." He ran a hand through his hair. "I'm not by any means a saint, Emeline. She was a fling. I've had quite a few, but I haven't been with anyone since the day I met you. It's like my dick deflates or something at even the prospect."

Emeline snorted. "You're very vulgar."

"It's because I want to do very vulgar things to you."

"Like what?" she couldn't stop herself from asking now that she felt a bit lighter from his explanation. One of the traits Emeline had already learned that Adam possessed was brutal honesty. She believed him.

"Like fuck you so hard, you'll still feel me inside of you when I'm done."

Her heart began to race frantically, but sex would not solve everything. They still had things they needed to work out, and the space between them seemed far greater than just standing a few feet apart.

"Why did you choose that moment in the office today to announce we were together?"

"Because I wasn't going to allow anyone to think badly of you."

"I was embarrassed," she admitted, "but it would have blown over."

"I've seen the toll that kind of strain can take," he answered quietly.

"You've had a relationship with someone you worked with before?"

He looked at her pleadingly, shame written on his face. "I never did relationships."

His confession stung. If he didn't do relationships, what the hell were the two of them doing?

"It was a fling, Emeline, and I told her that was all I was looking for and made no promises to her." He looked down. "She developed feelings for me, all the while gossip rang around the office. Some of her coworkers were awful to her, saying she got a promotion because she was fucking the boss."

"Did she?"

His head snapped up. "No! It was on her own merit." There was more. She could sense it even though he had stopped talking. He huffed out a breath. "I began flirting with another woman at work, one who had been cruel to her, knowing that it would get back to her. I thought … I thought it would be easier if she hated me, that if word spread about me being a womanizer, she'd get the sympathy, and I'd be the bastard." His face contorted then into anger. "I didn't ask her to have feelings for me. I didn't *want* her feelings."

"So you hurt her?"

"Yes!" he exclaimed loudly, then his voice softened. "Yes, but I never deceived her. I told her from the very beginning that a fling was all that would ever be between us."

"But you *did* deceive me."

Confusion marred his features. "How?"

"You never told me that we would only be a *fling*."

He crossed the few feet between them, and took hold of both her shoulders. His face was stunned. "You are not some fling, Emeline. Jesus, that's not what I've ever wanted with you."

"What do you want then?"

"My father … he…" Adam let go of her and then suddenly turned away and walked over to the couch and sat down, and placed his head in his hands. "No! I can't blame my father or use him to excuse my behavior."

Emeline stayed where she was. Was he finally opening up to her about his parents?

"We were happy once," he said softly. "My father, mother, and I were so happy. My father wasn't always rich, you see. His own parents lived practically hand to mouth until my grandfather built a profitable company. My father turned it into an empire, but he always taught me the value of a dollar and we never lived in excess. He loved his work and he had such passion for it, but more so for his family. We were happy."

"And it changed after your mother died." It wasn't a question. She felt the answer every day inside herself. She and her father were also once very happy.

Adam nodded, though still he sat in the same position on the couch. "The Cancer Families charity … I hadn't known my mother was sick, not for a very long time. She had wanted something good to come out of her illness, so that even if *it* took her life, cancer would never really win. My mother was passionate about helping the families of the stricken. She had said they suffer, too. The emotional part she couldn't fix, but the financial one she could help with. My father, after she died, never wanted to think of cancer or any other case he *deemed* hopeless, so he quit charitable donations all together, save for the few his accountants advised him to keep for tax purposes." He added the last part with disgust in his voice.

It made sense now. She remembered reading about Charmont Sr. ending all funding to charities he had created; only now she understood it to be due to his own grief. Emeline finally moved from her spot and sat beside Adam on the couch. Her heart was breaking for the little boy who had lost his mother. When he finally looked up at her, tears pooling in his eyes, her heart broke even more. He was opening up a wound before her, one that he had probably only sealed with a Band-Aid.

"She was in remission. I thought..." He inhaled deeply. "I thought she would be fine, but then not even a year later, it came back."

"How old were you when she died?"

"Twelve. God, I was sad all the time. My father, though, he became bitter and angry, ruthless even. He became cold and distant with me as well, dumping me on the housekeepers and butlers, leaving for long periods of times, but still, he was able to push forward in life, while I felt like I was constantly being drowned in darkness. I didn't want to be miserable all the time anymore, so I became bitter and angry instead, like him, and then suddenly life was livable again. If I no longer cared, I had nothing left to lose."

"But then your father died."

"And all I felt was numb." A tear rolled down his cheek, no longer trapped by its owner's iron hold. He took Emeline's face in his hands. "Don't you see? I can't bear the thought of someone hurting you, not Jarod, not vile office gossip. I haven't felt *anything* in a very long time, but you make me feel *everything*. I don't always know how to deal with all these feelings suddenly raging inside of me."

And now she finally understood all of him. She brushed the wetness off his cheek and brought herself closer to him. "I don't always know, either," she murmured against his lips right before she kissed him softly. "I was closed off, too, before meeting you. I even tried to fight my feelings for you."

"Because you were afraid I'd hurt you?"

"Yes."

"Never, Emeline. I swear it." He touched his forehead to hers, and they sat there holding each other for a while.

He had finally erased the doubt in her mind. He didn't say the words, but she knew. He loved her. She wanted to cross the final space, to forget that Jarod was still out there, to forget about the Sabines in the world and office gossip. They could save those problems for tomorrow.

"Now about those vulgar things…"

Chapter Eighteen

She was deliciously sore in all the right places when she awoke the next morning. When she rolled over, she expected to collide with Adam's hard body, hoping he would take her once more before work, but her hand landed on a piece of paper instead.

"Had something to do this morning. Didn't want to wake you. See you at work. Yours, Adam"

Yours. She definitely liked the sound of that.

She had to finally force herself out of bed, shower, and get ready for work. *Work.* Emeline groaned, knowing she would have to face everyone today. It didn't matter anymore. She'd go in with her head held high and show them she wasn't bothered by what happened yesterday. This wasn't high school, and Publishing Enchanted wasn't filled with people getting ready to stab you in the back. Add to that, the fact that she was already in her current position before Adam became her boss, the highest possible position in her department, so there could be no rumor or speculation of an unearned advancement.

And she wasn't going to let Jarod dictate her life either. The stupid Cupid had to have signed in downstairs and given some form of ID to prove who he was and which company he worked for in order to be admitted into the building. Today, she'd find out who he was and who he worked for, something she should have done yesterday, and then, if it turned out that it was in fact Jarod who hired him, it would only be another nail in his defense case.

Dressed, ready, and determined to see this day be better than yesterday, she grabbed her phone and keys, and headed out. She checked her phone quickly while waiting for the elevator. It was down to two percent since she forgot to charge it yesterday, but fortunately, she had an extra charger at work. She saw three missed messages, ten missed phone calls, and a whole bunch of texts. They were all from Adam. He had apparently been frantic yesterday when she left work and he couldn't reach her.

As she skimmed through the texts, not really wanting to relive yesterday considering all of it was moot now, she noticed a text that was *not* from Adam, one that came from a number she did not recognize. "I hope you enjoyed your gift yesterday. There is more to come."

Her hands were shaking by the time her elevator finally arrived. She'd definitely be calling Adam's detective friend today with all of this. Jarod had sent someone to call her a whore yesterday, and had the guy pass out tabloid magazines to her friends. God only knew what else he had in store for her. Adam had been certain that Sabine had not orchestrated those photographs to be taken. She hated the paparazzi and was often a victim of their smears herself. They lurked everywhere. Jarod could have simply seen the magazine and used it to his advantage, but Emeline feared that he himself had been the one to take the photographs and since he couldn't have known that Sabine would show up on Adam's doorstep, he could have been following Adam.

The thought chilled her to the bone. This was going to be something else she'd talk to the detective about.

She decided to hop in a cab instead of taking the train. She called Adam from the car, but there was no answer, and then her phone finally died before she could leave him a message.

When she got to work, Devon told her that Adam had called, saying he was running a little late. She breathed a sigh of relief. At least he was safe and she was sure he'd tell her about whatever it was he'd needed to do this morning.

She smiled at Christina and strolled into her office, leaving the door open. Christina didn't come in, apparently still giving her some space. She needed a few minutes anyway. This thing with Jarod was really taking a toll on her. Everything else she could deal with, especially now that she and Adam had worked things out.

Twenty minutes later, her emails were checked, a few of them answered. She walked over to Christina, who then immediately asked how she was doing. The poor girl had been holding it in, apparently. Rhonda, DeAnne, and Joe came over to them as well.

"I'm fine, guys. Really," she reassured them. And then, of course, she noticed the stares of other coworkers, but they were sympathetic rather than judgmental, so she decided to address them.

"Yesterday was a sick prank, played by an equally sick individual, and I am not going to dwell on it. I hope none of you will either." She would not be ashamed. She would stand up and fight to get her life back.

"As far as the tabloid," she continued, "Well, it was as Adam said—a piece of garbage."

"That girl ain't got nothin' on you, baby," Joe said.

His remark was followed by a few whistles, and she could have sworn she heard an "It's about time," from someone.

She shook her head and laughed at Joe's antics, grateful for him breaking the tension. And she was so grateful to the girls for stepping up yesterday to collect those magazines. She thanked them.

"We always have your back," Rhonda said.

DeAnne opened up her mouth to say something,

but then Emeline watched her eyes widen in surprise, staring at something behind Emeline. "Who is that?"

"Oh my God, is that—" she heard someone else ask.

Emeline turned around to see the source of everyone's current stares.

"Still a sexy beast," she heard DeAnne say.

It was Adam. She'd know that man anywhere, but now his hair was short. He still managed to keep his wild look, with the hair longer on top and fading to a close crop on the sides. She loved his long locks, but this also totally suited him. The thick beard was gone and replaced with something a bit more than a stubble.

Oh my God, he has a dimple in his right cheek.

She felt completely out of breath as he walked toward her, never once breaking eye contact.

"Hi," he said when he finally reached her.

"Hi," was all she could say back. It reminded her of their exchange after the first time they had slept together.

He held out his hand and she gave him hers. "My mother once told me that there would one day be a girl who would steal my heart. She also told me to make sure that I steal hers. I love you, Emeline. You've stolen my heart, and now I've come for yours."

He'd finally said the words, the ones she'd longed to hear, the ones she'd longed to say to him, but, somehow, they always got stuck in her throat. And then she heard the sharp intake of breath from various people around her as he took a knee in front of her and then pulled out a red velvet ring box. He opened it to reveal a diamond ring in the shape of a square, the light catching its brilliance, and she was sure that the other little diamonds around it made it even more beautiful, but she could barely see it. Her mind was focused on the hopeful gleam in Adam's eyes, and his beautiful face was all that she could see.

"Emeline Rose Bell, will you marry me?"

Last night had been a turning point in their relationship. He had finally opened up and let her all the way in, and now he was making himself completely vulnerable, opening himself up to the possibility of rejection. She only needed his courage to say the words back to him, to let him know that he already owned her whole heart and there was no one else she could have ever given it to. They had stripped each other of their protective armor and now there was none left between them.

She felt her heart about to burst with happiness.

Until she felt it stop…

Chapter Nineteen

Adam's mind was screaming, the noise deafening, while the shouting and chatter around him were nothing more than muffled sounds. A consciousness without a body was all that he was until slowly, parts of the outside world began to invade.

He became aware that the bastard was now dead, his armed security guard having taken him out, though a bit too late it seemed. Jarod lay dead, his eyes open, in a pool of his own blood, and the only remorse that Adam felt was that he would not get to kill the piece of shit himself.

"Focus," he heard someone gruffly say. And then he saw the blood on his hands, and on his new crisp white shirt that he had bought for this occasion this morning after he cut his hair and got rid of the forest that was his beard. "Are you listening?" the gruff voice said again. "More pressure. The ambulance is on its way." This time he recognized the voice as Joe's.

When he had woken up that morning, with Emeline tucked into the crook of his arm, he had never felt so free. The bitter and angry man he once was had been slowly disappearing since the day he was enchanted by a young woman he saw sleeping in a cemetery.

She had been under his skin since that day, and then slowly, every day since, she had melted the ice around his heart, so much so that he knew he didn't want to spend a day without her. Screw the restaurant and waiting nearly two more weeks for some arbitrary holiday, he had thought this morning. He was asking her today.

Memories of looking in the mirror after his transformation this morning flooded his mind. He had felt his pocket for the ring that once belonged to his mother and was hopeful she'd like both the ring and his new look, but if she didn't, he'd grow out his hair again, and buy her a new ring. None of that mattered as long as she agreed to be his forever.

He had strolled into the office without a care of what anyone else would think, and told her exactly what was in his heart. When he got down on one knee and gazed into her tear-filled eyes, he thought for sure she would say yes, that is until her entire demeanor changed into one of horror, and the whispered word "no," came out of her mouth instead, and was repeated in a scream. Nothing but confusion had registered at first, but realization was crashing down on him now, hard and fast.

She had flung herself at him, knocking him down.

"More pressure, Adam," Joe repeated. "Twenty-eight. Twenty-nine. Thirty. Come on, Emeline. Breathe, honey."

...And took the bullet meant for him.

Emeline wasn't breathing. She had no pulse. Joe, who thank fuck had been a lifeguard in his past life and was CPR certified, was working on her while Adam applied pressure to the wound.

If she left him ... God, if she left him ... he'd never resurface this time.

He ignored the chaos ensuing around him as the firefighters, paramedics, and police officers showed up at the scene. His sole focus was on Emeline and getting her to a hospital. Joe worked on her until the paramedics took over, but Adam stayed close. He needed to be beside her, to keep his hands on her at all times to prove she was still alive. They got her breathing, her heart beating at least, and then in a rush, they moved her.

"I'm fine," Adam snapped for the third time when an EMT suggested he get checked out.

They were downstairs and loading Emeline into

the ambulance and then he climbed right in after her, took one of her hands in both of his, and as the doors closed, he pleaded with her. "Please, don't leave me.

He finally had to let go of her when they carted her away to surgery. He heard a paramedic utter, "GSW," and "clean exit." That was good, he supposed, as well as the fact she was still alive. He would not give up hope, because that was all he had at the moment—hope that the universe would not be so cruel as to take away the thing most precious to him.

Edmund arrived a short while later, and he silently thanked whoever called her father, sparing him from uttering the words, "Your daughter has been shot."

"How is she?" Edmund asked him frantically.

Adam sat in the waiting room, along with many of the publishing staff, though he sat off by himself in a corner. "Still in surgery." His voice sounded flat and monotone, even in his own ears. "It should have been me in there."

He recounted what he had learned so far. One of his downstairs security team had supposedly called out sick that day and vouched for his replacement. He was found locked in a trunk just a little while ago, barely conscious with a nasty concussion. Jarod didn't act alone in this. He still had some sway it seemed with a few former shady clients, one of whom had helped him get the jump on the security guard. Jarod had then made his way up the service elevator, dressed in uniform. He'd already notified Timothy, the guard on the Publishing Enchanted floor, that he was coming up because Adam had requested extra security detail today, and since Adam had been unreachable, getting ready to propose to Emeline his sole focus, he'd missed the call from Timothy to confirm.

He was angry at Timothy for not being more

diligent, angry he had not used the professional security detail his father once used, angry at the world, but mostly, angry at himself that it was not him lying in that hospital bed instead of Emeline.

Surprisingly, Emeline's father did not agree with him. He placed his hand on Adam's shoulder. "I think we both know you would have willingly taken ten bullets for her, and she would have blamed herself for every one of them."

"How could she ever think that any of this was her fault?"

"How could you?" Edmund asked. "It's the fault of the man who pulled the trigger. She's going to be okay." Edmund released his shoulder and then finally broke down. "She has to be okay."

Adam nearly choked on his own tears watching Edmund sob. He had lost so much already, and now Emeline was all they *both* had left.

Sometime later, Adam blurted, "I was down on one knee, proposing to her when it happened."

Edmund widened his eyes. "Well, then she still owes you an answer, son." After a beat, he added, "Nice hair, by the way."

Son. Adam was touched by that and he'd hold on to the fact she still owed him an answer.

****

"God, baby, I was so scared." Adam didn't care that tears were pouring down his face as he brought her hand to his lips and kissed it repeatedly.

The bullet had missed her heart and anything vital. She was going to be fine. Edmund had left the room to call his family in Paris, but Adam also knew he was giving him a few moments alone with her.

"Me, too. Oh, Adam, when I saw him aim that gun at you…"

"Shh," he cooed softly. He didn't want her agitated now. The doctor had said she needed to rest. "He's gone, Emeline. He can't hurt us anymore."

Her lip quivered, and tears pooled in her eyes. "I didn't even get to tell you that I love you."

Adam gently cupped her face. "I already knew that." He smiled reassuringly at her.

"And I was about to give you my answer when we were rudely interrupted."

"Not funny, Emeline," he chided. "You do owe me an answer, but not now, Princess. I don't want to associate you getting shot with a marriage proposal. What would we tell our kids?"

Her brows shot up, but then she smiled and covered his hand with hers. "I'm alive, Adam. The doctors said I'm going to make a full recovery. And who knows how much time any of us get on this Earth? What I do know is that I want to spend the rest of all that I have left with you."

"I had a whole thing planned originally," he told her. "A fancy restaurant, violins, ring in the dessert, the works."

"You didn't?" She laughed.

"Too much?"

Emeline scrunched up her nose in response. "I would have loved it anyway." She ran her fingers through his hair, from the longer length to the closely cropped. "Fuzzy." Then she caressed his beard.

"You like it?"

She nodded. "I like seeing more of your face."

"You should get some rest," he told her. It seemed an effort for her to keep her eyes open. "I'll be right here."

"You can tell our kids you asked me when I told you that you've stolen my heart," she said. "I love you so much, Adam. Ask me again."

She was right. It didn't matter how, or where. All that mattered was that she was alive and she would consent to be his wife, his forever. He would not refuse her anything. "Will you marry me?"

She smiled widely, radiating her love for him. "Yes!"

He kissed her softly on the lips, tasting the salty tears belonging to both of them.

On their Christmas Eve in Paris, while lying in bed, tangled in each other's arms, Emeline had finally told him the story her mother used to tell her, about a little boy, trapped in a castle. He had been lonely and scared at first, but he tried to fight the witch. As he grew older, the fight in him died. He still heard the cackles, but they no longer scared him and his loneliness was his companion. The witch had faded away as a result, having lost her power over him, and only then did he truly have nothing, for there wasn't even anything left to fight.

Emeline went on to tell him about a young woman, who had many adventures. She, too, had been alone, but her travels were *her* companion. And on one blisteringly cold night, she had sought shelter in the castle. The weather, brutal, forced her to remain for weeks. She managed to befriend the young man, to slowly thaw out his heart until it burst with love for her.

When the evil witch returned, they had defeated her together, finally setting the boy free, and instead of a prison, they had made the castle a home.

It had been no wonder the little boy reminded Emeline of Adam. He had been trapped inside himself for so long with no sorrow, no fear, no fight left in him. He had forgotten how to live. And it was himself who had been the witch who cursed him. With Emeline, they had defeated her together.

Epilogue

Ten months later

"I now pronounce you…"

The first snow of the season fell the night before their wedding in December, blanketing the outdoors of their venue. The reception would be held inside, but Emeline still wanted the ceremony to be outside.

The air was calm, the temperature in the mid-thirties, and with the heaters positioned along the aisles, the guests could sit comfortably even with their coats open.

Emeline had ordered a faux fur shrug with a single clasp in front to wear over her dress. And like the year previous for the ball, she had found a dress she simply could not picture herself leaving the store without. The dress was classic and modern mixed into one, white with silk and lace, thick straps on the shoulder and plunging in the center, fitted to the knees and then flaring out. The train almost looked like a second piece, bunched in the back from her waist to the floor. She wore her hair in a loose up-do with a headpiece comprised of pearls and dangly jewels. The thing she cherished most, however, was Adam's mother's ring, now sitting on her right hand to make room for her wedding band on the left.

And then there was her Adam, still wild and breathtaking in his midnight suit and cognac-colored tie, to match her eyes, he had said. He had grown his hair out a bit, reaching to the center of his neck, but he kept his beard cropped close. His eyes shone as they were about to be pronounced husband and wife.

He had stared at her adoringly as she walked toward him down the aisle, following a trail of rose petals. Emeline's throat had felt thick with emotion as she gazed upon the man she planned to spend forever with.

He came forward, shook hands with her father, and then, never looking away from her, he led her down the rest of the way toward an arch with white and copper gauzy drapes. They had promised to love and cherish each other for the rest of their lives in front of friends and family.

"…husband and wife."

As the sun lowered, casting a yellow and red glow across the sky, he cradled her face in his hands, and kissed her. It started out sweetly at first, but it seemed neither could help but deepen their kiss, letting their tongues touch and twine until several people cleared their throats, while several more whistled and cheered.

"God, I love you," he told her when they finally ended their kiss. He still cradled her face.

"I love you, too. So much, Adam."

He then leaned in to whisper in her ear. "I'm going to do very vulgar things to my wife later."

And just like that, he managed to get her heart rate up. "Think anyone would notice if we skipped the reception?"

He seemed to ponder her suggestion. "Probably."

She shrugged her shoulders. It was worth a try. Maybe they could sneak off to the bridal suite at some point, she thought.

They turned to face their guests and walked down the aisle for the first time as husband and wife.

Together.

The End

THE BEAST IN A SUIT

www.elenakincaid.com

EVERNIGHT PUBLISHING ®

www.evernightpublishing.com